Terry Nation's

AVON

A TERRIBLE ASPECT

by Paul Darrow

Imitate the action of the tiger;
Stiffen the sinews, summon up the blood,
disguise fair nature with hard-favour'd rage;
Then lend the eye a terrible aspect.

—Shakespeare, *Henry V*

A Carol Paperbacks Book
Published by Carol Publishing Group

To Terry Nation--a great writer--
and to Janet, my wife, without
whose help I could not have
attempted to emulate him.

First Carol Paperbacks Edition 1991

Copyright © 1989 by Paul Darrow and Terry Nation

A Carol Paperbacks Book
Published by Carol Publishing Group

Editorial Offices   Sales & Distribution Offices
600 Madison Avenue   120 Enterprise Avenue
New York, NY 10022   Secaucus, NJ 07094

In Canada: Musson Book Company
A Division of General Publishing Co. Limited
Don Mills, Ontario

Carol Paperbacks is a registered trademark of
Carol Communications, Inc.

Manufactured in the United States of America
ISBN 0-8216-2503-9

10 9 8 7 6 5 4 3 2 1

Carol Publishing Group books are available at special discounts
for bulk purchases, for sales promotions, fund raising, or
educational purposes. Special editions can also be created to
specifications. For details contact: Special Sales Department,
Carol Publishing Group, 120 Enterprise Ave., Secaucus, NJ 07094

Prologue

In the fourth season after the wars for Uranus, he walked into the sanctuary.

I was eighteen years according to the Earth calendar and would never again meet a man quite like him.

Well concealed, I had watched him for some hours as his firm yet unhurried stride carried him towards me.

From time to time, he would disappear from view as clumps of rock and thick undergrowth hid his progress.

At other times, sulphurous mounds would cast grotesque shadows and these, combining with the prevalent heat haze, caused his outline to shimmer. It was as if he was a mirage hovering above the wilderness.

Some sixth sense warned me that his eyes, that would never be still and that would not miss anything, had already searched me out. It warned me, as I cowered in my hiding place, that this man, though he travelled through a strange and frightening land, had no fear of it or me.

While he was still far off, I told my mother of his approach. For the moment, she appeared unconcerned and continued her work in and around our cabin.

Constructed of Raphael teak, a wood as strong as iron, this was set into a solid rock face that hid it from above and all but masked it from prying eyes below.

1

The stranger came nearer, ever nearer, until I was able to see him quite clearly. Of average height and build, he was dressed in a black leather coverall and appeared to be unarmed.

I grew confident. I was equipped with a pump action gun and a twin-bladed knife with serrated edge. I was also familiar with this terrain. It was my sanctuary into which he had come. But, despite my advantage, my judgment of distance must have been faulty. All too soon, he was upon me.

I rose to my feet and pointed the powerful gun at him. No more than a few feet separated us. He stopped, stood very still for a moment, then turned to look at me. Was it my imagination, or did he smile? It was hard for me to tell, for my eyes held his and I found myself peering into deep, dark reservoirs of exhaustion and pain. The exhaustion that comes from the act of mere living and the pain of disappointment in the acts of others.

For all that, our visitor exuded a kind of menace that caused me, even in the intense heat of that day, to shiver with apprehension.

Neither of us spoke until my mother walked over to us and asked his name.

He seemed reluctant to take his eyes off mine, but now he turned them like twin lasers upon her. The intensity of his gaze caused her to step back in alarm. I pumped a charge into the chamber of my gun.

"Do you intend to shoot me?" the stranger asked.

"It's possible," my mother replied.

"Ah! Then the matter is open to discussion." This time there could be no doubt that he smiled. It was as if a bright light had been switched on or a cloud had scudded away to reveal the rays of a sun. But it was a smile that was soon gone and that might never have

2

been.

"Who are you?" my mother asked him again.

"My name is Avon."

I frowned. Avon was an Earth name and the Earth was the heart of Federation power.

"Where have you come from?"

Avon pointed to the sky.

"And where are you going?"

He seemed to have to think about that. "I don't know. Perhaps somewhere I have never been," he said finally.

"I am called Mara and this is my daughter Rowena," my mother said. "Do our names mean anything to you?"

Despite her show of confidence, I could tell she was afraid. My father had been killed fighting with the Dissidents in the recent wars and it was possible that this could be a Federation officer or a bounty hunter.

Avon seemed to read our thoughts. "I am not of the Federation," he said.

"How can we be sure?"

"You can't!"

He and my mother laughed.

"You are welcome here," she said.

I was surprised. She rarely welcomed anyone, but forced them to move on.

I looked once more at the man who had somehow succeeded in piercing her armor of distrust. He looked back at me. He reminded me of a great cat considering if it would be wise for him to enter another's domain.

For a while, it seemed as if he was about to reject the offer of hospitality. My mother, older and wiser than I, indicated that I should lower my gun. I did so and only then did Avon move. He followed her to our cabin.

Pushing aside the canvas cover, my mother ushered

him into the single room that ran thirty meters from east to west. After the brilliance of the day outside, it took some moments for our eyes to adjust to its semi-darkness.

Avon saw the fireplace at one end of the room and the two cots that my mother and I used for sleep at the other. His glance passed over our few sticks of furniture and came to rest on the hole at the base of the rear rock wall. He raised an eyebrow in enquiry.

"It's a well," my mother told him, "fed by a stream in the hills. It's good, clean water." She began to prepare food for us. "We were forced to move here from Phax's city," she said. "We're able to hunt for food and we brought with us an adequate supply of protein and vitamins."

Avon eyed my gun. "What about ammunition?"

"Limited, but Rowena is careful and accurate."

"I'm glad to hear it."

My mother nodded to me and I placed the weapon on a rack attached to the wall. Once I had done so, the tension seemed to drain out of Avon's body and I was able to see how tired he was. "Lie down," I said. "I will bring your food and water to you."

Avon sat on the edge of my sleeping cot. His back was to the wall. His field of vision covered the entire room as well as the canvas entrance. "Where is Phax's city?"

"A thousand kilometers from here. On the dark side of the moon," my mother replied.

"The moon?"

"Phax is one of eight moons that orbit the satellite Raphael." I interrupted. "Didn't you know you were on Phax?"

"I've run from the Edge of Uranus," he said. "I've lost my sense of direction."

4

"Are you running from the Federation?"

"Subsidiaries more like."

I shuddered. Subsidiaries were half-crazed female mutoids paid to hunt down important fugitives and to engage in other unsavory tasks.

My mother handed me food and a beaker of water. I passed them to Avon. "Are you a Dissident?" I asked as he devoured what I had set before him. He shrugged.

"You fought against the Federation?" I persisted.

"Yes."

"Through the wars for Uranus?"

"Yes."

"Have you killed many men?"

My mother gave me a look that seemed to forbid the question, but Avon answered it.

"Many men. Some women."

"Of the Federation?"

"What else is there but the Federation?"

I don't know why I asked the next question or how I knew what the answer would be. "Are you a Killer man?"

Avon looked at me sharply. "I was once."

I frowned. Killer men formed an elite group whose members carried out assassinations and torture on behalf of the giant Earth corporations. I turned my back on him and walked from the room into the outside air.

Darkness was gathering and the moons of Raphael were fading into temporary oblivion. They must have distracted me, for I did not hear Avon approaching me. He was as silent as a cat.

"By the light of one moon," he said, "you appear very beautiful. Imagine the effect created by seven."

Night fell like a black curtain and we stepped back into the cabin where my mother had prepared a bed

5

for him.

He washed in clear, cold water. Then he laid himself down and was instantly asleep.

We could have killed him then. We didn't and he knew we wouldn't.

The night time passed and, waking at first light, I could see that my mother still slept. Avon was gone.

I sprang from my cot and, not bothering to dress over the simple shift I wore for sleeping, I ran outside.

All the moons were full and gave off a light equivalent to that of two Earth suns. I was temporarily blinded.

When my vision cleared, I saw that Avon was standing in the shadow of a rock. His head was tilted to one side as he listened intently.

I approached him and his eyes flashed a warning. Then I heard it. The swish of rotor blades as they cleaved the air. The drone of a muffled engine.

Avon beckoned me into the shadows. "Heliplanes," he said. "Two of them flew past us heading west."

"Are they looking for you?"

"I think they've found me!" He smiled. This time there was no bright light, no hint of the rays of a sun. This was a smile like a shard of ice.

I noticed he was carrying my pump action gun. I looked into his eyes. They held a strange fire. His skin seemed alive, as if charged with an electric current. He quivered with excitement, reminding me of a great hound straining for the kill.

"I'll help you," I said, but my words were drowned as a heliplane suddenly appeared as if from nowhere. It roared into plain view directly above us.

Avon threw himself to the ground, rolled out of the shadows, rose on one knee and fired the pump action three times in rapid succession. Almost in an instant, he was on his feet. He fired again at the heliplane as its impetus carried it away from us. For a moment it seemed to hover in the sky like a gull, then it exploded in a ball of fire.

I gasped in terror, shock, excitement and admiration.

Avon took my arm and we ran to the cabin. "Protect Mara," he said. "Whatever happens, don't leave here." Then he was gone in search of the other aircraft.

My mother, rudely awakened, stood guard with me at the entrance to our sanctuary. There was silence.

We knew that heliplanes carried a maximum of three. Each one would transport a pilot and two Subsidiaries.

A shot rang out and splinters of Raphael teak splattered the room. I saw a Subsidiary dash from cover and charge towards the cabin, its giant strides eating up the ground.

Almost immediately, there was another blast and the creature exploded as if it was a canister of flammable liquid. Then there was a tremendous noise of firing and dirt and debris rose in clouds as pump action bursts scored the ground in front of us.

I took cover as best I could. I was shaking with a combination of fear and excitement.

The gunfire seemed never-ending.

My mother cried out as a rock splinter struck her face and I turned to help her. A second Subsidiary entered the cabin behind me. I whirled round and stared at it. I was frozen with fear. It was hideously scarred and its mouth was covered in a white foam like some rabid dog. It stepped towards me and I fell back in horror. Then it cried a terrible cry and crashed to the floor. A parabolic knife was thrust into the back of its neck.

Avon stepped nonchalantly into the room. "Are you all right?"

I nodded. He smiled and was gone again.

I ran to the entrance and watched him as he loped away to the west. There he would find the other heliplane and its pilot.

Within a short while, a column of smoke rose into the sky.

Some time later, Avon returned. He extracted the knife from the Subsidiary's corpse. "The pump action jammed on me," he said. "It was as well I had this." He smiled. He knew that I had thought him unarmed. "I'll get rid of this," he said and dragged the body outside.

My mother was unconscious, but not dangerously wounded. I bathed her cut face and, deciding not to move her, covered her with a thick animal hide to keep out the chill of the night.

The day went. Later, in deep darkness, Avon came to my bed. I did not protest when he removed my shift and lay down beside me.

I had never been loved before and I would never again be loved so well.

His mouth sought mine. He carassed my eyes, my face, my breasts, and his bitter perspiration mingled with mine. He entered me. Pain and pleasure commingled. Even as he burst within me and I cried out, I knew he had planted his seed. That I would mother his child.

Long afterwards, as Raphael's moons spread their fingers of light in anticipation of the dawn, we walked outside the cabin on the killing ground of yesterday.

"I must go to Phax's city," he said.

"Why?" I clung to him.

"I am the prey of many hunters. Sooner or later, they'll find me. There'll be a reckoning and I would prefer it to be on my terms and on ground of my

8

choosing."

"What if the Federation have taken the city?"

"I doubt that they have. Otherwise, we would be fighting Death Squads not Subsidiaries."

"If you go, I know I will never see you again." I said helplessly.

He smiled a sad smile. "I was a Killer man," he said, "for the corporations on Earth. I had a change of heart and mind and ran from them. They do not forgive easily." All the time he was speaking, his eyes scanned the sky and the wilderness that surrounded us. "I ran to Uranus," he went on. "It's an awful place." He shuddered.

"It has great mineral wealth," I said.

"Yes. It was a secret that was soon discovered. The Federation moved in and the wars began."

"My father died in those wars," I said quietly. "Once we heard of his death, Mara and I left Phax's city and hid here."

"We fought a great battle on the Edge of Uranus," Avon said as if he had not heard me. "We fought and lost. The survivors ran. Some went into the Beyond, where even the Federation does not dare to follow."

"Stay with me in this sanctuary," I said urgently.

"It won't remain a sanctuary for long. If I stay, they'll come for me. When they find me, they find you. I think you're too young to die!" He smiled. Then he took me back into the cabin and loved me once more.

I fell into a deep and dreamless sleep. When I awoke, Avon was gone forever.

When many Earth months had passed, the thought that he was dead came into my mind.

I cradled his son in my arms. "Your father is dead," I whispered. "Rogue Avon is dead."

The child was silent. He looked up at me and I saw

9

in his eyes the familiar darkness of disappointment and pain.

The boy was my whole Universe. He was Kerr Avon, the only son of Rogue. The Universe would know his name.

PART ONE

Rogue

1

The Federation had conquered Uranus and its satellites and ruled most of the known Universe. Its empire stretched to the rim of Andromeda, to the edge of the Beyond.

In celebration, it now assumed a benevolent expression and declared a new era of harmony and peace.

It allowed the cannon fodder of resistance to return to its former controlled, monotonous routine. Reprisals were few. Surveillance techniques were such that this majority could be effectively policed.

However, those who were thought to have the potential for leadership were ruthlessly pursued and captured or slaughtered.

The Federation death list grew smaller. This was a tribute to the efficiency of its Iron Guard, its Death Squads and any number of bounty hunters and Subsidiaries.

The Empire was vast. There was no escape. But one man alone is not easily found in a galaxy.

Rogue Avon ran, walked and crawled through the wilderness of Phax until, after many Earth days, he stumbled into the moon's city.

Gold, a timeless commodity, bought him food and a place to hide. It also allowed him to supply himself with weaponry and ammunition.

Arrogant in victory, the Federation had not yet seen fit to occupy Raphael and her moons. When Avon learned this, he obtained passage on a shuttle flight to the mother planet.

The people of this tawdry Uranian satellite were nervous with anticipation of the wealth and opportunity that an imminent Federation presence could provide.

Avon visited a brothel in the financial district of the satellite's seedy capital city. He met a whore called Gerasa.

She was beautiful, but she had the narrow eyes of a thief and a mouth like a razor blade. She took him into a squalid room and undressed. Standing naked before him, she eyed him curiously.

"I'm looking for somebody," Avon said.

"I've been looking all my life," she replied.

Avon smiled slightly and the prostitute relaxed.

"I don't have much time," he said. "I want to reach Federation space. I need someone to fly me there. For a consideration, of course."

Geresa licked her lips in anticipation of her share of that consideration. "You need Clay," she said. "But he's very expensive and only deals in gold."

"I have gold," Avon said quietly.

"A lot of gold."

"I think I may have enough."

The woman smiled sweetly, but her eyes glittered

with malice and Avon guessed what was about to happen.

The door to the room burst at its seams as two men smashed their way in. They were big and ugly and armed with machetes.

Avon turned to face them. He produced a twin-bladed knife with serrated edge. The two men hesitated. This was a mistake. Avon took the split second available to him and, with a flowing economical movement, slashed one of them across the throat. The intruder, choking on his own blood, emitted a horrible gurgling sound and fell to the floor. His companion, not to be disposed of so easily, parried Avon's thrusting knife with his machete. For a time, the two men were locked in a duellists' embrace.

Avon took a step backwards. He twisted the twin blades against the metal of the machete and tore the weapon from his opponent's grasp. The man stood quite still. He was staring death in the face.

Avon said, "You can go. Take that with you." He indicated the bloody corpse.

The man did not hesitate this time. He obeyed instantly, dragging the body through the remains of the shattered door.

Avon turned to Gerasa. She cowered in a corner of the room, trying to clothe her nakedness with a curtain draped over a window of dirt-streaked glass. Avon slapped her hard across the face and she yelped with pain as blood oozed from the corner of her mouth. "You shouldn't have done that," he said. "But now that the preliminaries are over, you can tell me where to find the man I need."

The whore tried to smile winsomely, but blood and fear masked any seductiveness. "I'll take you to him," she said.

13

Avon flung her clothes at her. "Get dressed!"

She obeyed hurriedly.

At Avon's insistence, they left the building by scrambling through the window. He was not anxious to risk meeting any more of her accomplices.

Gerasa led him through dark and narrow alleys that stank of the filth swilling in their gutters. They passed buildings that housed the downtrodden and abused. The homes of those without hope.

Eventually, she brought him to a low metal shack. It was situated in a district close by the moon landing complex where Avon had disembarked from the Phax shuttle.

The shack was cool and dimly lit. Its walls were papered with star charts. A man was sitting at a desk. He looked up as they entered.

"He wants a runner into Federation space," Gerasa said quickly. "He says he has gold."

The man at the desk smiled. "I'm Clay Gilpin," he said.

Avon said nothing.

Gilpin was slim and neat. He had an open, honest face. but, as always, the eyes are the clear windows of the soul. His were small, green and malevolent.

"Did her friends try to steal your gold?" he asked, his voice high pitched and sibilant.

"They tried. They failed."

Gilpin laughed humorlessly. "You stupid bitch!" he said to Gerasa. "Get out!"

The whore whimpered a protest, but his fierce glance silenced her. She smiled at Avon. Then she turned and left.

Gilpin sat himself on a rickety wooden chair and tilted it back against the wall. "Where do you want to go?" he asked, picking at his teeth with a sliver of wood.

"Earth."

Gilpin laughed. "Too far!" he scowled. "You look to me like a man who would always want to go too far." For a moment, his otherwise mean eyes twinkled with amusement, as if he wanted Avon to share a joke.

His visitor stood silent and motionless.

Gilpin said, "I can take you to Gamma 15. It's inside Federation territory, close to the Rings of Saturn. I have connections there. The Federation turns a blind eye to their activities. They've learned how far they can go without fear of reprisal. Far enough, but not too far. You're not like them at all." He sighed. "You can reach Saturn Major from there and then run to Earth."

"How much?" Avon asked, his voice a whisper.

"How much have you got?"

Avon smiled coldly.

"Five thousand credits in gold," Gilpin said.

"Two thousand."

Gilpin snorted. "Not interested."

"Three thousand."

Again Gilpin snorted and Avon turned to go.

"Four!" Gilpin called after him.

"Three and a half."

"Done!" Gilpin smiled broadly.

"When?" Avon asked.

"There's no time like the present."

Avon extracted a pouch from the weapons bag slung over his shoulder and counted out three thousand five hundred gold credits.

Gilpin scooped up the coins and placed them in a box which he shut away in a nuclear-proof safe buried in the floor. He eyed Avon approvingly. "I don't suppose there's any point in asking you where you got this

15

gold?"

Avon's eyes narrowed. "None at all."

"The spoils of war?" Gilpin persisted.

"Let's go." Avon said.

"Gilpin shrugged and the two men walked out into the night.

They rode a monorail to a sector of the shuttle base, then walked to a launch pad that held two aircraft. One was a sleek, four-seater, wide-decked speedship, the other was a rocket-propelled heliplane. Avon viewed this latter with some distaste.

Gilpin smiled. "We'll fly in this," he said and led the way into the speedcraft. Its flight deck was well furnished and comfortable. Its flight console was of the latest design.

"This ship is tuned to perfection," Gilpin said. "She can dodge anything out there." He operated a control and the pencil-shaped spaceship's hatch closed silently. He threw a number of switches. The engines fired and the throb of power caused the aircraft to shudder.

"Before we leave," Avon said, "there's something I would like to make quite clear. Try and cross me and you're dead!"

Gilpin laughed. "I believe you!" He pressed a button, the ship's computer came on line and rockets began to propel the craft upwards.

The machine hovered for a few seconds before slowly easing its way out of the minimal gravitational pull exerted by Raphael's atmosphere. It plunged into space.

Gilpin proved to be an expert pilot.

The ship's advanced, computerized radar screen was capable of warning him of the approach of any other craft that might prove hostile. It also informed him of the proximity of meteorite showers and space debris. As a result, their journey passed without incident.

In what is known as the Hollow Ground, between Uranus and Saturn's Rings, Gilpin placed the machine under the control of the automatic pilot, settled into his chair and promptly went to sleep.

Avon rarely slept. He remained watchful and wide awake.

The pilot slept the sleep of the just. Or the conscience-free. He did not wake until they reached the rim of the Hollow Ground, close to the Outer Rings. It was as if a personal, accurate alarm had roused him.

He threw a switch and a picture of the space outside glowed on a video screen. Gradually, the picture became clearer and Gilpin pointed out various important areas of the star plan. In the far distance, he pointed to the outline of a tear-shaped asteroid. "Gamma 15," he said. "I'll be picking up some contraband, ready for the good life when the Federation is running Raphael and the moons. Once we've landed, you're on your own."

"I wouldn't have it any other way." Avon replied.

Gilpin smiled, then looked innocently puzzled. "Who are you?" he asked.

"You wouldn't want to know."

"Have you fought against the Federation?"

"Hasn't everybody?"

Gilpin brought out a liquor bottle and offered Avon a drink. He took a long gulp himself.

"I swim with the tide," he said. "If you swim against it, you're in danger of drowning." He sighed and took another drink. "I envy you."

"Why?"

"You'll die well. As for me? I'll be shot in the back in some dingy hole on a half-forgotten planet."

"At least it will be quick," Avon said.

17

The pilot scowled and drained the bottle. He tossed it aside and turned his attention to the ship's controls.

Carefully, with great skill, he guided the speedcraft underneath Gamma 15's radar screen and ground-hopped into the interior of the satellite.

Gamma 15 was a man-made, barren landscape blasted out of Saturn moon rock by Federation engineers.

It was little more than a staging post for trade, legitimate or otherwise. There was no evidence of a military presence. The army was confined to the radar listening positions that Gilpin had so cleverly evaded.

The local authority was a small, corrupt police force. From one of its officers, Gilpin acquired papers that would assist Avon's travel plans.

"I thought I was on my own?" Avon said.

Gilpin smiled. "I've changed my mind. I think you need all the help you can get."

The pilot then took him to see a forger and persuaded him to "doctor" the police papers so that they would be untraceable. Finally, he booked Avon onto a freight shuttle that would carry him to Saturn Major. On Saturn there would be Starships capable of reaching Earth.

Gilpin bade him farewell and it was clear that he regretted their parting. He smiled and said, "I'll read about your death some time."

"We all die, it's just a question of when," Avon replied. He handed Gilpin a gold piece worth five hundred credits.

The pilot hesitated before taking it. "I'll put this with the others," he said. "Maybe they'll breed!" He wrote a name on a scrap of paper. "This is someone who will help you when you get to Saturn. I'll telegraph ahead and tell him to expect you."

"Thank you."

"If you walk and fight alone, you're sure to die alone," Gilpin said. "Don't tell me! You wouldn't have it any other way!" He laughed.

Avon's best recollection of him would be that hollow, joyless laughter.

The two men parted and Avon took the shuttle to Saturn Major. He found it very different from the slums of Raphael and the wilderness of Phax.

Saturn's capital was a modern hi-tech city. Its inhabitants were sleek and sophisticated. Their environment was well policed, so that the lower grades had limited access to the Alpha, or the privileged grade's fleshpots.

The military was well represented. It was clear that the occupation force for Raphael and her moons would launch from here.

Avon, heavier and bearded since his time on Phax, had only little faith in the paper bribed from the police officer on Gamma 15. Once again, he used gold to provide his requirements.

When he had familiarized himself with his surroundings, he chose to make contact with the man named on Gilpin's scrap of paper.

The man was called Pruth. He lived in a small house in a quiet protected suburb. He was an historian who lectured at the Saturn Alpha Military College. One of the training grounds for future Federation officers. A typical Martian, he was large, of indeterminate age and had a full, chubby face with a clear complexion. His eyes, bestriding a bulbous nose, were browless and fire red.

He greeted Avon warmly and seated him in a room furnished with antiques from the second calendar. He plied him with good food and fine wine.

Avon ate and drank sparingly, ever watchful in case

19

his host's bonhomie should change to malice or threat.

Pruth spoke in a Martian dialect that was taught as a specialized subject at various schools on Earth. It was used by the Killer men as a code.

The teacher did not seem surprised that Avon understood him.

"Clay Gilpin says you are a man who might be of use to me," Pruth said.

"I was under the impression he thought you could be useful to me."

If Pruth had had eyebrows he would have raised them. Instead, he went on, "Gilpin is a mean creature, but his word is as good as an oath. He thinks I can trust you." He smiled evilly. "Even if that trust should turn out to be misplaced, I doubt that you could harm me or survive my displeasure."

Avon said nothing.

Pruth continued, "If you will do something for me, I am willing to return the favor. This is called a fair exchange."

Still Avon said nothing.

The Martian sipped wine from a crystal glass. "I hold a high and influential position here, but it is precarious. In the past, I have not exactly seen eye to eye with Federation policy. Now, I'm sure you will have noticed the military buildup here. In the wake of the military will come the investigators." He paused for effect. "So far, Saturn has been left to its own devices but, since the expansion of Empire, perhaps because of it, there is some intolerance in the corridors of Federation power. I have enemies there."

"Why?"

"Well, helping someone like you won't endear me to authority."

"If that's the case, why bother?"

"For the cause."

"What cause?"

"The cause of freedom from oppression."

Avon sighed. "I don't think I blame your enemies for their intolerance."

Pruth looked at him sharply. "Don't you love liberty?"

Avon snorted. "I'm not sure of the meaning of the word, but, whatever it is, it's a pipe dream in this Universe."

"Dreams can come true."

"So can nightmares."

Pruth shook his head. "We're getting nowhere. The only cause you seem to espouse is your own."

Avon stared at him unblinkingly. "I'm as good as dead. I'd like to choose the time and place, that's all."

"You're a pessimist."

"Which means I'm rarely disappointed."

Prush laughed. "We must beg to differ."

Avon smiled coldly. "What can I do for you?"

The historian drained his glass. "Gilpin thinks you carry yourself like a trained killer. He has an instinct in these matters. I want somebody dead."

Avon's face was expressionless. "Life is cheap, but I'm expensive. What can you offer in return?"

Pruth smiled thinly. "The papers you have may or may not be good enough to get you to wherever you want to go. Earth isn't it? You have a sentimental streak. You want to die at home. However, I can produce documents for you that will pass the closest scrutiny. For a while at any rate. I should add that Gilpin's contacts on Gamma 15 are not too reliable and the satellite's forgers are not as expert as those to be found here in Saturn Major."

"I might be prepared to take a chance."

21

"I doubt that. You seem to me to be a careful man. Besides, I know that you are Rogue Avon, that there is a price on your head and that you are on the run. If I know it, others will soon find out. Including Clay Gilpin. His reward would be quite handsome if he were to inform the Death Squads of the forgeries you are carrying. You can't be certain he won't betray you."

Avon remained impassive. "Why should I trust you?" he asked.

"Because it would be very easy for me to betray you. The fact that I have not already done so should inspire you with some confidence. And I need you to do this service for me."

"What will the murder achieve?"

"By removing an associate of mine from the scene, I will be saved some embarrassment when the Federation investigators come to call."

"What is the victim's name?"

Pruth glanced at him in genuine surprise. "I thought you would have guessed. Clay Gilpin!"

There was a long silence. The Martian broke it at last. "You may wonder how I know about you. I was impressed by your admirable self-control when I revealed my knowledge. Gilpin telegraphed me news of your arrival and gave your general description. I fed the relevant information into a personal computer. Remember, I'm a respected official of the military college and have access to such things. I learned a lot. You confirmed your identity to me when you clearly understood and could speak this dialect. Knowledge of the language is one of the accomplishments noted in your file."

"It's my turn to be impressed," Avon said as if he wasn't.

"Impressed enough to do what I ask?"

"Gilpin doesn't have access to this information."

Pruth grimaced. "He'll get it. It will take him a little while perhaps, but greed will encourage his persistence."

"His papers have got me this far," Avon said.

"You have been fortunate so far!" The Martian settled in his chair and studied Avon through steepled fingers. "You face a dilemma. To coin an ancient phrase, you are between the devil and the deep. I think your best bet would be to throw in your lot with the devil."

Avon stood and faced him. "There's a nice irony to the situation," he said.

Pruth smiled. "Gilpin has handed to me the instrument of his own destruction."

"Is he still on Gamma 15?"

"Yes. He will remain there until I tell him otherwise. I'll send him a telegraph stating that you have agreed to join with us in our contraband schemes. He will be quite unsuspecting when you return to him."

Avon said, "It shouldn't take more than a few Earth days to kill him and then come back here. Once I've completed your task, what's to stop you handing me over to the authorities and claiming any reward for yourself?"

Pruth made a dismissive gesture, then smiled disarmingly. "Nothing! This is when mutual trust comes into play. However, to ease your mind, I will provide you with fresh documentation before you leave. You see? I am prepared to give you something that can be used in evidence against me should you feel betrayed."

"Will Gilpin have backup?"

Pruth seemed surprised by the question. "No. He will be alone."

Avon paced the room like a cat.

Pruth poured himself another glass of wine. His hand was unsteady.

Avon stopped pacing. "This seems a little too—how shall I say?—a little too contrived for my liking."

"A happy coincidence that permits the satisfaction of our mutual requirements."

"I don't believe in coincidence," Avon said acidly. "How shall I kill him?"

"I leave that to you."

"I expect you require proof of his death?"

"Naturally."

Avon smiled, but said nothing.

The Martian leaned forward. "I want his eyes. Bring me his green eyes." Pruth's own eyes glowed flame red.

2

Avon left the Martian's house ostensibly to prepare himself for his return to Gamma 15 and the assassination of Clay Gilpin.

In reality, he melted into the overpopulated, rundown section of Saturn Major where prostitutes, pimps and other human debris congregated.

Once he was alone, he permitted himself a wry smile at the tutor's amateurish behavior.

Avon had been around too long and had been betrayed too many times to be easily taken in, and Pruth, for all his intellect, had been less then beguiling.

Avon thought he understood the system that was being worked with Clay Gilpin.

Many of the fugitive from the wars for Uranus would find their way to Raphael and her moons where

Gilpin's team of informers, such as Gerasa, would point them towards the pilot so that he could assess their worth in bounty, alive or dead.

Any "runners" of whom Gilpin was not sure he would pass on to Pruth. The Martian's computers would do the rest. Then, pretending to be of assistance, he would send them back to Gilpin for annihilation or capture. Provided, of course, that he had established they were worth the effort.

Pruth had tried a subtler gambit with Avon. The attempt to convince him that he was being hired to kill the very man who would undoubtedly seek to kill him was a clever touch. But not clever enough.

Avon wondered how many fugitives had had to die to pay for Pruth's extravagant life-style and Gilpin's sleek spacecraft.

Avon paused for thought.

It would seem that none of the papers he had so painstakingly acquired would be of any use to him now. He could hardly afford to trust Gilpin's forger and it was a cast-iron certainty that he could not trust the Martian.

His one chance of returning to Earth would be to fly himself there, and in order to do that he required a space vehicle. The one person capable of providing him with one was Clay Gilpin.

Avon, who rarely missed anything, had watched closely as the pilot had brought them into Gamma 15 and he felt sure that, with the aid of the on-board computer, he could control the ship alone.

However, the distance involved would be a problem. Gilpin's machine, though modified, could never be expected to reach Earth without further adjustments and extra fuel. He could not afford the time for the former and dared not risk attempting to secure the

25

latter.

He made a swift calculation. With clever handling and some luck, he might manage to pilot the craft to within the Clouds of Magellan where any number of Earth satellites, man-made and launched into Earth orbit in the previous century, could provide him with other means of completing his journey.

Having made up his mind to pursue this course of action, he set out for the Saturn Major shuttle terminal. He would return to Gamma 15 and claim Gilpin's spacecraft. He was quite prepared to kill the pilot to get it.

He again permitted himself a smile when he realized that Pruth's influence allowed him to move freely in the planet's capital. It was when he reached the satellite that his real problems would begin.

As he expected, the flight passed without incident and the shuttle set him down among the gloomy outbuildings of Gamma 15's landing station.

Almost immediately, it took off again, the blast from its lifting rockets causing a miniature dust storm and a vibration that shook the shabby service area.

Avon passed through the security cordon without difficulty and made his way to the docking bays in search of Gilpin and, more important, his spacecraft.

He found them both in what appeared to be an otherwise deserted building and the pilot greeted him like a long-lost friend. A reaction that put Avon momentarily off his guard.

"Pruth telegraphed that you were coming back," Gilpin said enthusiastically. "You impressed him. He thinks we can work together."

Avon said nothing, but his eyes searched for the pilot's inevitable backup team.

Gilpin caught his mood and frowned. "What's

wrong?" he enquired.

Avon, attempting to appear more casual than he felt, leaned against the nose cone of the spacecraft and gave his potential adversary his complete attention.

"The Martian sent me to kill you," he said, smiling like a crocodile.

For a moment, Gilpin seemed taken aback, then he laughed his high-pitched laugh. "I knew you were a rare man," he said, "but now I know you are an honest one."

Avon said nothing, but his eyes were as black as pitch. He exuded an air of menace.

The pilot's laughter faded and he braced himself as if to repel an assault. Avon did not move a muscle.

Gilpin's green eyes narrowed. "You won't find it easy to fulfill the contract," he said.

Avon said, "I must be worth quite a lot for you to be going to so much trouble."

Gilpin snorted. "Less than some, a good deal more than others." He assumed a sly expression. "Congratulations on catching on so quickly."

Avon shrugged. "It wasn't difficult. You're an amateur at this game."

The pilot stiffened. "You're very confident," he said. "Perhaps too confident!"

Just then, two Subsidiaries emerged like wraiths from the interior of the spacecraft. For a moment, there was a terrible stillness.

Very slowly, Avon shifted away from the nose cone and turned to face them. Then, in no more time than it takes to blink an eye, he ducked under the machine and rolled into a position that placed the body of the ship between him and his adversaries. He guessed they would not dare fire on him for fear of hitting Gilpin or the spaceship.

27

He unsheathed his twin-bladed knife with serrated edge. This would be a silent encounter.

The first Subsidiary made a serious error. It ducked after him wielding a vicious-looking scimitar, but Avon had no difficult parrying its wild slashing motion, and his hard fingers curled round the creature's throat while his knife plunged into its stomach and twisted upwards into its artificial heart. It wailed like a banshee as it died.

Avon smiled grimly. He was right when he considered Gilpin an amateur. But amateurs could sometimes make an unexpected move.

He crept slowly along the outer wall of the building, making sure that he stayed in the shadows.

Suddenly, the lights went out and there was an almost complete darkness. Only the gray outline of the spaceship was at all visible.

Avon stood, his back to the wall, his body tense and waiting.

He did not have to wait long. The other Subsidiary came at him from the side and Avon gasped as its scimitar gashed his left arm and drew blood.

A cloud of agony clutched at him but, with a supreme effort, he braced himself against the wall and flung himself forward. He and the Subsidiary crashed to the floor. The scimitar locked between the twin blades of his knife, the Subsidiary's foul breath gushing into his face, Avon slowly forced its head back, the fingers of his bloody left hand gouging its eyes.

After a few moments, the Subsidiary breathed no more, but Avon administered the coup de grace, slashing it across the throat.

Two down and one to go. Maybe!

Avon tried hard to control his heavy breathing and, with a piece of cloth ripped from his tunic, formed a

28

tourniquet that halted the flow of blood from his arm. Blood that poured through the fingers of his hand.

Gilpin's laugh broke the stillness and invaded the dark. "Come out, Avon, wherever you are!" his voice taunted.

Avon spat blood. For an amateur, the pilot wasn't doing too badly. But now he was alone. Or was he?

Avon waited. If nothing else, he had the patience of a saint.

Besides, he had guessed, and guessed right, that he was worth more to Pruth alive than dead. He would wait.

It seemed an eternity, but could not have been more than a few minutes, before the lights flashed on again and Gilpin, in a more reasonable voice said, "This is very silly. Why don't we face each other? I'm sure we can come to a satisfactory arrangement!"

Avon thought it was time to move. Reversing the tactic that had drawn the Subsidiaries to him, he rolled back under the nose cone, sprang to his feet and, having gauged Gilpin's position from the sound of his voice, flung his knife like a javelin. It struck the pilot in the neck and he went down as if he had been poleaxed.

"Like I said," hissed Avon through gritted teeth, "an amateur!"

It was Gilpin's turn to spit blood. "If you knew, why did you come back?" he gasped.

Avon conquered the pain in his left arm and withdrew his knife. The pilot screamed in agony.

"You made a mistake," Avon said. "Now you have to live, or rather die, with it."

The green eyes flashed. "I'm not dead yet," Gilpin said and, with a superhuman effort, raised himself to his feet. He swayed for a second then, with what was almost a swagger, turn his back.

29

A single gunshot rang out. Gilpin, like a gymnast executing a slow fall, drifted to the floor. Dead before he got there, he had fulfilled half his prophecy. He had been shot in the back in a dingy location.

Avon whirled round. At the entrance to the hangar stood the whore, Gerasa. Her gun was pointed at him.

Avon smiled. The woman shuddered and the weapon fell from her nerveless fingers. With the grace of a ballet dancer, Avon scooped it up.

The woman started to cry.

Avon, unaccustomed to tears, stood quite still, undecided as to whether to shoot her or hand her back the gun.

Gerasa dried her eyes, sniffed and gazed at him as if he were a visitor from another planet. Which, of course, he was.

Avon handed her the weapon. the elation he had felt after dealing so effectively with Gilpin and his Subsidiaries was gone. He had merely postponed the good day on which he would die.

Gerasa tried to be coy. "I don't have much to offer," she said, "but you can have it if you'll take me with you."

"You don't know where I'm going," he said.

"It makes no difference."

"Why did you kill him?" Avon asked, indicating Gilpin's corpse.

The whore didn't answer.

"Were you supposed to finish me off if they couldn't manage it?"

She nodded.

"What made you change you mind?"

Gerasa moved close to him, placed her arms round his neck and stared into his eyes. "Surely you don't have to ask," she said.

30

Avon pulled her even closer. They kissed savagely. He took her there and then, on the dank floor of the hangar, amidst the blood and debris of the fight. She gasped and went limp beneath him like a rag doll. Avon dragged her to her feet. He caressed her neck. "You may die with me," he said. "Do you realize that?"

She shook her head and smiled.

Almost immediately, she proved her worth to him by stooping to Gilpin's body and performing a rapid search of the pockets of his tunic.

With a hiss of triumph, she produced a small plastic card with numerals and digits printed on it. "His computer card," she cried. "You can control this spacecraft with it." She handed it to him.

Avon frowned. He couldn't get over the fact that his demolition of Gilpin's plan had been achieved with relative ease. Perhaps Pruth was cleverer than he had given him credit for.

He took out his twin-bladed knife and it glistened in the neon light from above. He stooped and cut out Gilpin's green eyes.

The whore didn't flinch or move a muscle, merely watched, fascinated.

"For the Martian," Avon said. "Proof of Gilpin's death." He looked at her steadily. "What was your arrangement with him?"

"Who?"

"Pruth."

"I don't know him."

"But you were in on the deal with Gilpin!"

"Yes."

"Passing on fugitives who might be worth something?"

"Yes."

"Sticking with me won't be so profitable."

31

She shrugged.

Avon studied the computer card, then handed it back to her. "You placed it in the computer," he said. "I'll wait outside."

Gerasa did not move, but Avon saw the furtive look that clouded her eyes.

"How long have you and Pruth been planning to do away with Gilpin?" he asked casually.

She laughed and it was almost infectious.

"He told me you were likely to be the cleverest of them all," she said.

Avon studied the card. "I take it this would cause an explosion once placed in the on-board computer?"

She nodded.

Avon sighed. "Now what?"

"Pruth wants you to take Gilpin's place."

"You mean, until I outlive my usefulness, as he did?" he said, indicating the body.

"Something like that."

Avon crossed to the entrance to the hangar and looked out. "Did Pruth arrange that no one would interfere with what was going on in here?"

"Yes."

"He has considerable influence."

"Yes."

Avon smiled wolfishly. "A pity!"

"What is?"

"Before I left his house, I placed a miniature phosphorous mine in a location where he won't find it. It will explode in about twelve hours. He should be asleep, so he won't feel a thing."

For a moment, the girl seemed to doubt him. Then she laughed. "In which case, I'm making the right decision in going along with you," she said.

Avon threw Gilpin's eyes at her feet. "You might as

well have these."

She picked them up and put them in a pocket of her blouse.

"Where's the genuine computer card?" Avon asked.

She studied him for a moment. "How do I know I can trust you?"

"You don't."

She seemed to make up her mind quickly and extracted another card from Gilpin's tunic. She handed it to him.

Avon climbed into the space machine and swiftly refamiliarized himself with its interior. Very carefully, he placed the card and the ship's computer came alive.

The question, "Command?" flashed on its screen.

Avon punched in "Prepare for flight" and the machine flashed back, "Very well."

Avon made his way to the hatch and jumped to the ground, then made his way to the mechanism that would operate the hangar doors. "Will anyone try and stop me leaving?" he asked Gerasa.

"No. Pruth's influence will hold good. Until he dies, that is."

"Which gives us twelve hours. Maybe a little more," he said as he opened the hangar doors. "Get aboard!" he added.

"Where are we going?" Gerasa said.

"It's a mystery tour."

"I don't like mysteries."

"Well, you're going to have to live with this one."

"Or die here and now?" she asked.

Avon did not reply. He didn't need to.

They climbed aboard and he instructed the computer to close all hatches, to taxi outside the hangar and, once in flight, to set a course that would clear Gamma 15's orbit and bypass Saturn Major's space lanes.

Through the cockpit video window, he could see that the landing area staff were showing some curiosity in his activity. He order the computer to maximize its efficiency. In other words, to get out of there fast.

The machine complied. The spacecraft's vertical takeoff rockets flamed and activated and, creating a vibration to match that of the shuttle that had brought Avon to Gamma 15, it lifted off, increased speed and was launched.

"Truly," Gerasa asked, "where are you going?"

"Truly," Avon replied "I'm going home!"

3

Gamma 15's defense system picked them up immediately and a video telegraph ordered them to return to the shuttle base or face the consequences.

Avon, strapped into the pilot's seat, Gerasa peering anxiously over his shoulder, remembered how Gilpin had brought them in to the satellite.

He flew the spacecraft as low as he dared, given the contours of the landscape, and exhorted the computer to give maximum power. The machine responded.

Faster and faster, the spaceship hurled itself through the satellite's gravitational pull, as if it had discovered a life of its own. As if it was a huge and powerful dog that had just been unleashed.

Avon took a full video scan. Nothing.

Once clear of Gamma 15's orbit, he took another. This time, he saw four fighter ships in line formation taking up the pursuit.

He changed course, weaving and diving the machine

in an attempt to throw off the fighters' radar trackers.

Although modern and well equipped, the fighters had not been as tenderly cared for as had Gilpin's ship. Gradually, it drew away, leaving its pursuers floundering in its wake.

Avon sighed and wiped the perspiration from his brow. "Gilpin certainly knew how to look after his spacecraft," he said. "Of its type, this is one of the best I've flown."

"But will it get us to Earth?" Gerasa asked.

"What makes you think we're going there?"

She shrugged. "Gilpin and Pruth seemed to think that's where you wanted to end up. I didn't believe anyone could be so foolish. Now I've met you, I'm not so sure!"

Avon checked the fuel gauge. They were on half tanks. "Damn!" he said. "We'll be lucky if we get beyond Saturn." Then an idea struck him. He turned to the girl. "We'll have to free fall through the Drift," he said.

She looked bemused.

"The Drift," he went on, "is a space corridor between Jupiter's moons. We can switch off all engines and slide through it. It's a series of simple currents that will allow us literally to drift into the Clouds."

"Where?"

"The Clouds of Magellan. You can see the World through them."

"I still don't know what you're talking about."

"There are man-made satellites in the Clouds. We can reach Earth from one of them."

"But we still have to get there?" she said.

"Right!"

"What about Saturn Major?"

Avon thought for a moment. "If we assume that

35

Pruth's death will not put them on to us immediately and if we also assume that the Federation troops on Gamma 15 didn't feel they had any urgent reason to report our escape, then, and only then, we should be able to swerve round the planet without interference."

"That's a big 'if'!"

"Yes." He smiled.

"And Saturn's Rings?" she asked.

"We'll curve round the edge. That way, we can save fuel by using them as a glide path."

"You seem to have thought of everything."

"I'm good at improvisation."

She smiled back at him.

"Can you improvise an auto pilot for this ship?"

"Later, maybe."

She stared at him for a long moment, then moved to the back of the ship, undressed and lay naked on a bunk. Like a contented child, she fell asleep almost at once.

Avon instructed the computer to navigate and to activate all alarm systems. He swivelled in his pilot's chair and studied the woman.

She was nearly perfectly proportioned. He guessed her to be about one and three-quarter meters tall. Her body was deeply tanned, her pretty oval face framed with a mane of jet black hair. Her eyes, when they were open, were piercingly blue. Her breasts were rounded and full, her sex soft and inviting beneath a firm, flat stomach. He thought she could be no more than twenty-five years old.

He felt a stirring in his loins as he gazed upon her, but he turned away and studied the flight console instruments, all the time wondering how she had become involved with Gilpin and Pruth and their pathetic attempts to get rich quickly.

He knew that, once in Earth's orbit, he would be dealing with professionals. The Federation elite would not be so easily outwitted.

Gerasa slept a long time. The spacecraft had navigated Saturn's Rings and was well on the way to Jupiter's Drift before she awakened.

She stretched her body like a luxuriating lioness and looked at him, her long eyelashes hooding her sapphire eyes. "How safe are we?" she asked.

"Safe enough. We've by-passed Saturn and there's no pursuit."

"As you thought!"

"Yes." Avon frowned. "It's easy. Too easy. Almost as if whoever my enemies are, are deliberately holding back. Waiting to kill me on ground of their own choosing."

"Earth would be your choice too, wouldn't it?" she asked.

"Yes."

"Then all we have to do is pass the time until we get there." She beckoned to him.

He went to her and climbed into the narrow bunk.

She took him fiercely, as if she were a bird of prey and he was her victim. Her breasts were pliant beneath his hands, her lips moistened his, her legs and arms entwined him. He burst inside her, emitting a long groan of pleasure. But she was not satisfied and forced him to love her again.

When they had finished, she licked the perspiration from his neck.

"If you're going to die," she said, "I can think of worse ways to go!"

The alarm system sounded. They were approaching the Drift.

Avon sprang to the flight console and, having set a

37

master course, switched off all power.

The spacecraft shuddered, slowed and fell like a snowflake through space and time. It was as if nothing existed, save the ship and the impenetrable darkness outside.

Anxiously, they waited for the Drift to end, when Avon would reactivate the engines on full thrust and they would charge into the Clouds of Magellan in search of the satellite that would be their last staging post before Earth. The real danger would begin there.

4

The Clouds of Magellan appeared like giant mushrooms on the video and Gerasa's sharp intake of breath as she saw them confirmed her fear.

Avon spoke to her softly as he guided the spacecraft onto a course that would take them through a narrow gap between the two biggest Clouds.

"There's nothing to be afraid of. We've conserved enough fuel to get us through. Once within the Clouds, our radar scanner will select a satellite where we can land." "Where we can land in the middle of a Federation Death Squad, you mean?"

"It's possible, but unlikely. These satellites are sometimes deserted, having outlived their usefulness. Otherwise, they are manned by scientists. Pirates or robbers would find nothing of interest to them. Besides, they would know that, this close to Earth, the Federation would soon get on their track and hunt them down."

"Do you think the Federation will be monitoring us?" she asked.

"Undoubtedly. But they don't know anything about us. We're not flying a warship, so they are unlikely to intercept unless someone on the satellites reports our presence. They'll be curious, little else."

"all right, do what you have to do." "Strap yourself in," he commanded. "We could be in for a bumpy ride."

Gerasa obeyed and Avon gunned the engines.

The spacecraft shook and rattled as the Clouds clutched at it.

One moment, they thought the vibration would cause the machine to break up, the next, they were floating free in the area of calm between the stormclouds.

They floated for a long time while the computer scanned for satellites.

Occasionally, Avon would gun the engines so that they could move into a different computer waveband. This caused them to use up more fuel than he would have liked.

At length, a blip appeared on the screen and Avon instructed the computer to home in on it and prepare to land on the satellite it undoubtedly represented. As always, the computer obeyed, but warned that fuel was dangerously low.

Slowly, almost gingerly, the spacecraft maneuvered itself between the huge, scudding Clouds and soon it was possible to make out the satellite on the video screen.

Avon studied the computer facts. They revealed no sign of life and indicated that the surface below was sand and rock.

"I think we're about to land in a desert," he said.

Gerasa shrugged. "Wonderful! A pity you're not as good a navigator as Magellan was."

"Who?"

"The Clouds are named after him."

Avon looked at her sharply. "How do you know?"

"I haven't spent all my life on Raphael," she said innocently, but she turned away from his steely glance.

The spaceship altered course. Its rockets, stuttering through lack of fuel injection, backfired and the machine belly flopped into an enormous dune, its impact throwing up great clouds of sand. Particles rattled on the hull like rain.

Avon switched off all power. The silence that ensued was like death.

Once the sand had settled, there appeared to be no movement outside the ship.

Gerasa coughed drily. "What do you have in mind?" she asked.

Avon looked at her steadily. "I have in mind that there is more to you than meets the eye."

She blushed.

Avon extracted the plastic digital card from the computer.

"It was pre-programmed, wasn't it?" It wasn't really a question. "No wonder it was so easy to slip away from Gamma 15 and Saturn. I was meant to come here."

Gerasa clapped her hands like an excited little girl. "At last, you've caught on!" she exclaimed. "You're like a tortoise who has tried to convince everyone he's a hare!"

Avon smiled a deadly smile. "I would remind you that the tortoise won the race," he said.

"This race is over," she replied as she switched on the video scanner.

As the camera slowly turned, Avon could see that the spacecraft was surrounded by Federation troops. In the midst of them, smiling benignly, stood the Martian,

40

Pruth.

Avon turned back to the girl. She pointed a gun at him.

"Unlock the hatch and let them in," she said harshly.

Avon did not move.

"If you shoot me," he said, "all your efforts will have been for nothing. Pruth wants me alive."

Gerasa scowled at him. "Do as I say!"

"Tell me why?" he asked.

"I'll let Pruth do that."

Avon sighed. A sigh that seemed to suggest he had given up the ghost.

Gerasa relaxed somewhat, but the gun was steady in her hand.

"Pruth wanted Gilpin out of the way," she said, "but you knew that. I'm sure he'll thank you for killing him and for furnishing proof of his death." She extracted the pilot's green eyes from her pocket and tossed them on the console. "With Gilpin dead," she continued, "there is nothing to link Pruth with any illegal activities on Saturn Major or the satellites." She smiled. "Pruth knew you were a resourceful man. Knew you would find your way, if not to Earth itself, then as far as here. With a little help from me and a piece of plastic, you've proved him right."

"Why not kill me on Saturn and be done with it?" Avon asked quietly.

"And allow the Lords of Saturn and some obscure Death Squad officer to milk the credit?" She laughed. "Of those who survived the wars for Uranus, you were the biggest prize. By delivering you to the Federation in such a spectacular fashion, here in the heart of its power, Pruth has proved his genius. There will be nothing to stop him securing more and greater power to himself."

41

"And you intend to ride his coattails?"

"Well, I've not done badly so far, have I?"

"What will they do to me?"

She shrugged. "There'll be a show trial. The business corporations, your former employers, will approve of that. Then they'll blind and imprison you so that you can be brought out from time to time to illustrate the futility of resistance. You'll be a constant reminder of Pruth's strength and cunning."

"I would never have guessed I was so important," Avon said.

"You're too modest." Gerasa fluttered her eyelashes as if she was flirting with him. "You were the last to escape from Uranus. With the Federation Empire expanding, your capture will cause anyone intending to fight it to hesitate. And he who hesitates is lost!"

"You still haven't persuaded me to open the hatch."

Gerasa moved closer to him, the gun still unwavering in her grasp. She leaned over to throw the hatch switch herself and, in the split second that her attention was diverted from him, Avon smashed his elbow into the master power control. At the same time, he chopped down onto the woman's gun arm with the hard edge of his hand.

Two things happened. The last dregs of fuel in the spaceship's tanks ignited a jet stream that blasted the Federation guards standing in its path. Their screams of surprise and agony penetrated even the thick metal covering of the machine.

Simultaneously, Gerasa's gun fired, but its projectile thudded uselessly into the roof of the cockpit.

She fell to the floor, Avon on top of her. For a while, she struggled like a maiden trying to protect her most precious possession. Then she relaxed as Avon took her in his arms as if he were embracing her, even loving

42

her. His arm folded around her neck and, with one clean jerk, he snapped it like a reed.

Gerasa's head lolled to one side; her tongue was jammed between her teeth, her features formed a hideous smile of death.

Avon laid her body on the floor and quickly glanced at the video screen.

Apart from incinerating any number of guards, the jet stream had stirred an angry cloud of sand that swirled around the spacecraft.

Avon seized the moment. If he couldn't see any guards because of the miniature sand storm, they couldn't see him.

Clutching his weapons bag, he forced open the cockpit hatch and sprang from the spaceship. Soft sand broke his fall, but fierce, gritty particles lashed his face. He stumbled away from the machine, ready to eliminate any guards who might stand in his path.

He remembered from the video scan that there would be a group of high sandstone rocks to his left. It was most likely that the Federation Death Squad had been concealed among them and that their heliplane transports would be grounded there.

He knew that the spacecraft was between him and Pruth and any surviving guards and hoped that, with the element of surprise, he could kill the pilots before they knew what or who was hitting them.

Battling the twisting sand, he staggered and crawled his way until, as the sandstorm began to subside, he reached the rocks.

He was right, there were six heliplanes standing in line with only their pilots to protect them.

One of them saw him immediately, but Avon's black garb caused him to resemble a Death Squad officer and, while the pilot hesitated, he shot him with a full pump action blast.

Other pilots, confused by the melee at the spaceship and surprised to find themselves under attack, milled around the planes. Coolly, Avon shot them all. They fell like ducks in a gallery. Then, there was a further silence of death.

Avon reloaded and walked among the bodies, kicking them to see if anyone was left with a spark of life. No one was.

He looked back towards Gilpin's spaceship. Ten or a dozen guards were moving around it. Clearly, they had not heard the gunshots above the receding noise of the jetstream and sandstorm. He had a few minutes to spare.

Avon ran from heliplane to heliplane and tossed a delayed action phosphorous grenade into each of them save one. This last, he climbed aboard and, after swift refamiliarization with the controls, he started it up and the powerful rotors began to turn.

He knew that, as he lifted off, another sand cloud would form and the guards on the ground would fire at him in vain.

The plane jumped vertically like a flea and Avon guided it towards the spaceship. The guards, hidden by the agitated sand, were somewhere beneath him.

He flew over the machine that had brought him to this satellite of death and, as the sand cleared once more, he saw Pruth standing on a dune, staring up at him in a kind of wonderment, as if he were a visiting god.

Avon unleashed a god's wrath. He fired a fragmentation rocket at point blank range. It struck the Martian in the chest and blew him to pieces.

Just then, the phosphorous grenades exploded in the other heliplanes and a ball of fire swept over the sand towards the prostrate Federation guards.

Avon turned his machine towards the spaceship, its open cockpit hatch clearly in his sights. With great precision, he launched another rocket and smiled with satisfaction as it plunged through the hatch and blew the ship apart.

Then, he wheeled away and, the satellite possessing no gravitational pull to delay him, sped from the scene.

5

The heliplane handled smoothly and was well fueled. It was larger than those he had destroyed on Phax, because it was designed to carry troops.

But Avon knew it had a limited range and that, consequently, there would be a mother ship. The heliplane's radar would be homed in on her.

He threw a switch and a blue light flashed at him. He swiftly calculated that the larger ship was positioned some two hundred spacials to his right. Avon turned the heliplane to the left.

He flicked through the radar channels until another flashing light indicated the position of a man-made satellite within range. He set a course, safe in the knowledge that no one would pursue him. For the moment.

Soon, he approached the satellite. Quite different from the one he had just left, it was small and compact and seemed to consist of granite mountains. Lakes glistened amongst them.

The heliplane was mounted on wide skis. He would set it down on water, certain he would find a quay at the lakeside.

He banked the aircraft, reduced speed and glided it between two massive rocks. Then he straightened it and its rotors hovered it and it lowered, like a bird, to the still surface beneath.

As he had anticipated, Avon saw a quay and motored towards it. A solitary figure stood upon it, waiting to greet him. There did not appear to be any armed guards in the vicinity.

He steadied the controls and slowly docked the aircraft before bringing it to a halt.

Through the glass dome of the cockpit that resembled the eye of a huge insect, he studied his reception committee of one.

The man was tall and dark-skinned, dressed simply in gray coveralls that matched the color of his crinkly hair. He did not appear very old, but he was not young.

Avon suspected he was a satellite Guardian. A specialist who had volunteered to live alone on the man-made sphere to nurture and protect whatever it was the Federation required from it. In other words, the satellite would be a huge storehouse of material and Avon was about to confront the storekeeper.

He stepped from the heliplane onto the metal quay.

The two men stood apart, silently regarding one another for a long moment. Then the dark-skinned Guardian stepped forward, extended his hand and said, "I know who you are. I am Mishka."

Avon accepted the handshake.

"You're quite safe," Mishka said.

"How many times have I heard that!" Avons aid wearily.

The dark Guardian laughed. "I mean it. I've jammed the radar of the Starship that's hovering out there." He

46

indicated the atmosphere. "It's quite true that Federation obstinacy will discover your whereabouts eventually. But this is the last place they'll want to look."

"Why?"

Mishka frowned. "I don't think you want to know."

Avon said testily, "Satisfy my curiosity!"

"This is the Graveyard." The dark man watched closely for Avon's reaction. There was none.

Avon had heard of the satellite. Every Federation citizen had. It was here that the wealthy stored their dead. The dead who had expired of whatever cause, including hideous, contagious diseases.

No member of the human race could tolerate the silent recrimination of these dead. Curious, considering that the advances of science and the brutality of Federation rule had jointly refined the meaning of the word horror.

Avon was not prey to the superstition and awe that Mishka seemed to expect of him. He was unaffected by the fear that infection might breed in the very air of the Graveyard.

As if reading his thoughts, Mishka said, "There is no danger of infection. I've lived alone here for nearly twenty years and the only disease I'm suffering from is advancing age."

Avon smiled. "We all die. One way is as good as another, I suppose. I'm not afraid."

Mishka and he walked from the quay towards a substantial building set against the rock face that overlooked the lake.

"It's not unpleasant living here." Mishka said. "It's very quiet and peaceful."

Avon smiled.

"Also, there isn't anybody who is able to disagree with me."

Avon laughed.

The Guardian pushed a button and a steel door slid back to reveal the interior of the building.

They stepped into a long, clinically clean room that contained the minimum of furnishings. Mishka indicated doors that led to bathroom, galley and food stores.

"The main mortuaries are set into the mountains," he said. "Bodies are shipped here every Earth quarter. The next shipment is due in a month."

Avon shook his head. "It would be better to burn them on Earth."

Mishka smiled. "The wealthy, who have everything in life, are ever hopeful that, one day, there will be found a cure for death."

"You mean, the bodies are preserved?"

"Yes. In ice. The interiors of these mountains are giant cold stores. That's why there are so many artificial lakes. I need the water from them for the freezing process."

One wall of the room held a large video screen. Mishka noticed that Avon was staring at it.

"That's my communication screen," he said. "I've already been asked if I've seen your heliplane on my scanner."

"Why should you protect me?" Avon asked.

"I didn't volunteer to be the Graveyard Guardian," Mishka replied, "and I didn't take kindly to the Federation method of persuasion. This is my way of biting back."

"What have you heard about me?"

Mishka smiled broadly as if enjoying a huge private joke. He moved to a cabinet set into the wall nearest the door, extracted bottles of rare cognac and poured Avon a drink.

"I've heard your name," he said. "I've heard that a bounty of ten million credits has been offered for you. I've heard that a famous hunter and Killer man has promised to deliver you to the Federation Council for trial. So far, you've given them a good run for the money. In the end, of course, they'll get you. Alive or dead. It's up to you."

"I take it you don't want to try for the ten million?"

Mishka smiled again. "What would I spend it on here? Besides, I think you'd make the attempt extremely difficult for me."

"I'm having difficulty understanding why someone in the Federation is going to so much trouble," Avon said.

Mishka handed him another drink. "There's a split in the Federation hierarchy—a schism. Consequently, there's a lot of power playing going on. One party requires a spectacular coup to ensure its dominance. You're it!"

"So, I'm a pawn in someone's great game?"

"In a way. You're not much, but you're the best they've got."

"Thanks."

"You're welcome! The more difficult you make it for them, the greater the kudos when you're finally caught."

"Or killed?"

"I imagine they'd rather take you alive. But I don't think they're too fussy."

Avon thought for a moment. "Which group is trying to take control?" he asked.

"Pel Gros, Makarov, the Martian called Pruth. . . ."

"Pruth is dead."

Mishka looked at him sharply. "I'll take your word for it."

"Go on."

49

"Axel Reiss is another."

Avon sighed. At last, it began to fit into place.

Mishka paused, caught by the rapt look on Avon's face.

"There are others," he continued, "and there is little doubt they will succeed. You're the sacrifice that will aid that success. You obviously know why."

Avon looked at him and Mishka was appalled by his defeated expression. His eyes appeared sunken and opaque. His face seemed like a death mask.

"Reiss and I were Killer men for the corporates." Avon said quietly. "When I ran for cover and sanctuary on Uranus, a contract was put out and Reiss took it up. I never thought he would have the chance to fulfill it. After all, it was possible I might die in the wars. One of the reasons Uranus fell so easily was because all support and sympathy on Earth was crushed by Reiss and others like him. The corporates raised him up and he's trying to climb even higher. Also, he wants to exact a kind of revenge on me." He shrugged. "He wants me dead."

"Why?"

Avon seemed lost in thought. "It's very personal."

"Indulge me a little. How personal?"

Avon smiled sickly. "We share the same mother. Axel is my half-brother."

Mishka hastily poured another drink. "Sometimes," he said, "I believe in gods who play destructive, fiendish games with us. You seem to be a part of their devilish plot."

Avon stood, walked to the open door and gazed out over the placid lake. "It's a plot that will be resolved very soon." he said. "But not here. On Earth. Axel wouldn't want it any other way. Question is, how do I get there?"

"No problem."

Avon turned sharply, his eyes glistening. Mishka was alarmed by the sudden change, by the menace that exuded from his guest.

"I can launch you in a Pod," he said drily.

Avon laughed. A Pod was an orbital coffin. Shaped like a bullet, it could penetrate Earth's atmosphere and plunge to the ground without breaking up. Its only controls would be a direction finder and a small steering wheel. It would literally perform as if it were a projectile fired from a gun and, though small, it would be sturdy enough to crash land on any suitable surface. Water, or sand or snow.

"The way this satellite orbits," Mishka said, "I can fire you into the North."

Avon nodded. It would be snow.

The Guardian smiled. "You'll probably freeze to death before they find you. It's ironic—I could do that for you here."

Avon did not share the joke. "They'll find me." he said.

"And then?"

"And then, I'll die as well as I can."

Mishka shook his head, almost in disgust. "You're out of another century. Death is death. There's nothing noble about it."

Avon stared at him, but it seemed to Mishka that he was looking straight through him.

"It's better to live for one day like a lion than for a hundred years as a sheep." Avon said.

The dark man placed an arm on his shoulder.

"I have a terrible feeling, your day is about to end!"

6

The Guardian took Avon inside the mountain.

Hollowed out and spartan and clean, it contained thousands of transparent plastic bags, the bodies inside them preserved with tightly packed ice.

The bags hung from the walls and from the ceiling like twinkling icicles in a subterranean cave.

In a way, it was startling. As if they were strolling through a fairy grotto.

Avon didn't believe in fairies.

"It's a considerable waste of space," he said.

Mishka grinned. "That's something we have plenty of. Although the Federation always wants more."

They passed through a corridor into a small rock-bound hangar which contained a single Pod.

"You understand what I intend to do?" Mishka asked.

"I think so."

The Guardian scowled. "Not good enough! Listen to me!"

Avon listened.

"I'll switch off all cooling systems except the one required to prevent the Pod from breaking up in the heat generated by reentering Earth's atmosphere. Once through the gravitational layers, the machine will fall to the ground. It's likely it will go into a spin.

"You must activate the air vents which will affect the Pod as if it were held back by parachutes. It will then land reasonably gently. Once in the snow, because that is where you'll be, the machine is useless. Except as a shelter. The area in which you'll find yourself is desolate, cold and inhabited by Steljuks. Do you know what they are?"

Avon nodded. "Nomadic barbarians. Half man, half monster."

Mishka nodded in his turn. "You should get on very well together," he pronounced drily. "Within a few Earth days," he continued, "the Federation will surely have tracked you down. This is where you die." He paused. "As you have only a few days left, that's all the supplies I will allow you." He tossed a plastic carton of food into the Pod. He looked thoughtful for a moment. "In the unlikely event that you are taken alive," he said pointedly, "I'd appreciate it if you didn't mention my part in this."

"They won't take me alive." Avon said.

"I believe you."

Avon smiled shyly. "Of course," he said, "the fact that I will have penetrated Earth's defenses will not look good on Reiss's record."

The Guardian shrugged. "Killing you will make up for that. They'll parade your body for everyone to see. That'll cause some rejoicing among the Council members. Reiss will be their champion and hero."

"A somewhat tarnished hero." Avon said.

"That's a fairly accurate description of yourself."

"You're quite right," Avon said. "If I'm honest, I think Reiss should do well as one of the leaders of the Federation. He has the talent, the brutality, the intelligence, the ruthless ambition."

"You make him sound like the student most likely to succeed."

"I thought we were agreed that that's exactly what he is?"

"You also make him sound like you!" The dark man's

53

eyes twinkled. "Die well, Rogue Avon. Sooner or later, we'll all join you."

With that, Avon shook his hand and climbed into the Pod.

Mishka closed and sealed the hatch so that Avon could no longer see him.

Suddenly, the machine was filled with light as the hangar door slid back and Avon could see the sun glittering on the lake outside.

Almost as suddenly, the Pod began to move. Rocking back and forth, it shook him like a pea in a pod. He smiled to himself as he considered the pun.

However, he was cushioned somewhat by the padded satin lining of the orbital coffin. Then, with a high-pitched shriek, the launching mechanism functioned and the machine was hurled into the air.

It was as if a stone had been catapulted and the Pod behaved exactly like such a stone. As it reached the zenith of its climb, it hesitated, then plummeted faster and faster until it was travelling at such a speed that Avon could not distinguish what was outside his cocoon.

As the Pod entered Earth's atmosphere, it slowed and he could see the fires on its outer hull. Fingers of flame clutched at the machine. Then, with a suddenness that was as exhilerating as it was alarming, they were into the sky above the World and they accelerated.

As instructed, Avon took his cue to operate the air vents and the Pod floated downwards, as if supported by invisible parachutes, just as Mishka had described.

With a heavy thud, the machine struck the ground and half buried itself in a mountain of soft, brilliantly white snow.

Although chill, the Northern sun shone. It was a beautiful day.

All around him, Avon noticed that the blanket of

snow formed itself into grotesque shapes. It allowed no
growth, appeared to support no life. Even its brief
flurry of disapproval of his arrival had quickly subsided. He was in the middle of nowhere and there was
nothing and no one to comfort him. He shivered,
despite the sun.

Overcoming the fear that seemed to cramp him, he
forced himself to eat some of the food the Guardian
had provided. Then, having checked and cleaned his
weapons, he settled down to wait.

In a while, someone would come. Either attracted by
the noise of the landing, or by the sight of him just sitting there in the open as if on a picnic. Whoever it
might be, Steljuck or Federation Guard, he would be
ready. The good day to die was not far off.

7

It was the time of the White Nights and there was no
darkness, just a softening of the brilliance of the sun
and a hint of dusk.

Two full Earth days passed and nothing disturbed
him or the silence in which he dwelt.

On the third day, a small mammal appeared as if
from nowhere, studied him for a second and scurried
away. Not far off, it stopped and looked back at him,
cocking his head on one side. It was not alarmed,
merely bemused by his presence.

Avon thought to kill it for fresh meat, but decided
against it. He was getting soft and he knew it. There
was a time when the death of others was a matter of
indifference to him.

The creature, apparently reassured by some telepathy between them, went about its business. It burrowed into the snow, scratching for the food that was hidden from it.

Fascinated, Avon watched. It was as well that he did. Suddenly, the creature froze, its ears twitching in perfect accompaniment to its nose.

Avon stood, stared into the sky and listened intently. When he looked back, the animal, wiser by far than he, had gone.

Then, he heard it. The soft, far-off drone of an aircraft. Probably a heliplane; it was a big one by the sound of it.

He climbed into the Pod. The hatch still open, it resembled a tank with Avon peering out of its turret.

The heliplane was a troop carrier. Like a giant moth, it fluttered its way towards him.

Some two hundred meters distant, it hovered then settled on the ground, its rotors kicking up a snowstorm reminiscent of the sand blast he had created on the man-made satellite.

By the time the snow had settled, the machine, its engines silent, seemed to eye him in much the same way he had eyed the small mammal.

The plane's hatch opened and a man appeared. He dropped lightly to the ground and started to walk towards the Pod.

Avon readied the pump action.

The man approached cautiously. When he was within fifty meters, he stopped and removed his steel helmet that was emblazoned with the insignia of the Iron Guard. He shook his head to release a mane of black hair. He stood quite still.

A humanoid of average height, he was dressed in a black coverall with a silver ammunition belt tightened at the waist. He was armed, as Avon was, with a twin-bladed knife with serrated edge. He carried a pump action. His face was thin and pale. Fleshier round the jowls than Avon's, it was a face that bore a startling resemblance to his. But the eyes of his visitor, set in hollow cavities, were dark and expressionless. It was as if they had been carved from jet or black ivory.

The two men looked at each other for a long moment. Avon smiled.

Like a cat on hot metal, he leapt onto the surface of the Pod, raised the pump action and fired a devastating burst into the open hatch of the heliplane. For a second or two, nothing happened.

Then, with a roar that would have outdone a pride of lions, the machine exploded. A pillar of flame pierced the sky, pursued by a mushroom cloud of smoke and debris.

Avon's visitor had not moved a muscle.

Again, the two men watched each other as the noise from the destruction of the heliplane subsided.

The man stepped forward. Avon reloaded the pump action and took aim. The man kept on walking.

When he had drawn close, Avon lowered the weapon and dropped from the outer hull of the Pod to the ground.

"I've been expecting you," he said.

"So I understand." The other man smiled, but his eyes remained dull and expressionless.

"It's been a long time," Avon said quietly.

The other man turned and glanced at the burning remains of his transport. When he looked back, any hint of a smile had disappeared.

"You're making a habit of doing that," he said drily. "You have killed a good pilot and wrecked a superior vehicle."

Avon shrugged. "It's possible you could have had heavy backup."

Again he was favored with a humorless smile.

"What now?" Avon said.

"I think perhaps, it's your move."

Avon laughed. "You've chased me across the known Universe, from Uranus to Earth, and you're prepared to let me decide how to end it?"

His visitor stood very still. It was a long time before he answered.

"I'm glad you realize this is an end."

"Yes, Axel, but for whom?"

Axel Reiss, who was Avon's half-brother, nodded sagely. "You could have killed me just now. Why didn't you?" he asked, as if genuinely interested in the answer.

"Under similar circumstances, would you have killed me?"

Axel Reiss did not reply.

Avon thought for a moment. "I assume you have to take me alive or return with proof of my death?"

Reiss took a deep breath. "Yes."

"There's no other way?"

"Is there ever?"

"Then, so be it." Avon threw his pump action into the snow and took out the twin-bladed knife.

After a moment, Reiss followed suit.

Two two men faced each other, crouching in the familiar stance of the knifefighter. Warily they circled each other.

Reiss lunged to Avon's left, but his thrust was easily parried as sparks flew off the knives.

Avon side-stepped, feinted to the right, then slashed at Reiss's stomach. The other man backed off quickly and appeared to stumble. Avon was after him like a flash, but this too was a feint and a serrated edge glanced off Avon's arm, reopening the wound he had received, so many moons ago, from the Subsidiary on Gamma 15. He gasped with pain.

Reiss whirled like a dervish, leapt into the air and delivered a kick at Avon's head. Reacting sluggishly, Avon was struck in the temple and went down.

Reiss stepped back and Avon rose unsteadily to his feet. The blood that filtered from the wound in his arm was weakening him. He slashed wildly at his opponent, but to no avail.

Slowly, steadily, like a jackal moving in on a wounded lion, Reiss stalked him.

Avon was breathing heavily. The pain was almost unbearable. He was nauseous and perspiration was clouding his sight.

With a chilling cry, Reiss, as swift as a shadow, ducked under Avon's guard and buried his knife in his chest. He twisted it in the flesh like a bayonet, then withdrew it.

Avon fell to his knees, his life's blood staining the white snow a glittering red. He looked up and Reiss slashed him across the face.

With a deep sigh, Rogue Avon toppled forward.

The last thing he saw before he died was the small mammal who was studying the fight from afar.

Once again, there was the silence of death.

PART TWO

Rowena

1

Although they had shared the same mother, the respective fathers of Axel Reiss and Rogue Avon were very different.

The first man had been powerful in business and had exercised an almost equal power in Federation politics. He had envisaged Axel's career among the ranks of the Killer men as merely a stepping stone to higher things.

Once his woman had reached an age and condition that no longer pleased him, she was lain aside and, in time, passed to another.

This second man was a fiscal genius employed in the Federation banking system and had worn himself out at an early age. Lonely and jaded, he was a shell of a man. He lived only long enough to father his child and bestow his name.

Because of some atavistic fraternal conscience, it was Axel who guided the privileged education of his half-brother and ensured his enlistment among the Killer men. This elite was a private army of assassins and trouble shooters for the wealthiest corporations on Earth and in the known Universe.

Both Axel and Rogue became expert. The only difference between them was a matter of temperament.

Rogue Avon grew tired and was sickened by his work. For Axel Reiss it was a sublime vocation.

Reiss succeeded where Avon could be said to have failed. But a Federation future is never secure and, unknown to Reiss, Avon had left a legacy. The half-brother who had killed him would have to face the wrath to come.

Even now, his infant nemesis, far away and far out of time, was starting on the journey that would lead to their bloody confrontation.

On a dark night, in that half-forgotten place, Avon's son, Rowena and Mara received a visitor.

At first, the two women were wary of him and inclined to force him away. Then they remembered his legend and recognized him as the one who was known to wander the wilderness of Phax and who haunted the mountains to the North in a never-ending quest for gold, or some other El Dorado of the soul. He was called the Prospector.

A giant of a man, his face was lined with age and burned by the many moons of Raphael. He had startling blue eyes. His long gray beard caused him to resemble a famous prophet who might have inhabited a childish religious imagination.

He had been hurt in a fall and Mara tended him. He sat quietly as she anointed his wounds with a soothing unguent. His blue eyes, like perfect diamonds, held those of the child.

The child had reached four Earth years. He sat on

61

the edge of Rowena's sleeping cot and stared unblinkingly at the giant.

After a while, the Prospector frowned and looked away. The child did not move.

Rowena placed herself beside him on the cot and embraced him with a protective arm. "This is my son," she said.

The Prospector smiled briefly. "He's an unusual child."

"In what way?"

"He has the eyes of a hunter."

Rowena glanced at her mother who was standing by the gun rack. There was a silence.

"I don't mean to offend you," the Prospector said hastily.

All the while, the boy had not altered his gaze. His attention was concentrated on the old man. Then, suddenly and without a word, he extricated himself from his mother's arm, climbed from the cot and walked to the canvas door. He turned and smiled and went outside.

A kind of menace had departed the atmosphere. Or so it seemed to the Prospector and he visibly relaxed. "I'm sorry," he said, "there's something about him that is a little unnerving."

"You make him sound like a specter or a devil," Mara snapped irritably.

The Prospector said nothing.

Rowena had followed the boy to the door. She glanced outside. Her son was standing by the dune buggy that had brought the old man to them. She turned back. "Have you sufficient fuel to reach Phax's city?" she asked.

The Prospector nodded.

"Will you take us there?"

The man glanced at Mara, then looked searchingly at Rowena. "Do you really want to go there?"

Rowena shrugged fatalistically. "There's no alternative. The boy can no longer be raised like a wild animal. He must be taught civilization."

The Prospector smiled broadly. "The Federation rules Phax's city," he said. "A token force as it happens, but all that seems to be required. The people of this moon have blended all too easily into the system. I wonder why you haven't received a visit from a Coordinator or from the Iron Guard?"

"They've chosen to pass us by," Mara said. "We have very little to offer them."

The big man glanced at Rowena. "I wouldn't be too sure of that. However, I doubt that there is any real danger at this time. The Federation is pursuing a policy of tact and diplomacy."

Both women smiled.

"I won't ask about the boy's father," the Prospector continued. "You're right, of course. There is no life for the child here. None for you either. How old is he?"

"Four, almost five, Earth years." Rowena said.

"I thought he was older."

Neither woman made any comment.

The giant stood. His head almost touched the ceiling. "I'll take you to the city. But you must move on from there as soon as you can. You should seek anonymity. Ignore the system and trust that it will ignore you."

"We're grateful for your help," Rowena said.

"Don't worry about us," Mara interjected. "We'll survive. We have so far."

The Prospector looked at her solemnly. "The boy has to go farther."

"We intend to make sure that he has every opportunity to go as far as he is able," Mara said pointedly.

"When may we leave?" Rowena asked.

"In a few days, when the season of the sand winds is over. Once we reach the city, you should take the shuttle to Raphael and, if possible, move on to Saturn Major. There is a kind of civilization there. You will need travel papers. Do you have them?"

Mara moved to a cache sunk into the teak wall and extracted a pouch containing various documents. She handed them to the Prospector.

He studied them. "Very good," he said. "I don't think I've come across better forgeries."

"They're not forgeries," Mara said, "they're genuine papers, issued by the Federation, that I've adapted for an occasion such as this."

The Prospector laughed.

"Before we came here," Mara continued, "before the wars for Uranus, we were respectable citizens. I don't suppose the Federation documentation system has altered too radically."

"Not at all," the old man said. "These will allow you to reach Saturn Major without hindrance. Of course, they may not be good enough to assist you to your ultimate destination."

"Where might that be?" Rowena asked cautiously.

"Earth, I imagine. The boy was clearly fathered by an Earth man."

Neither woman spoke. The child entered, brushing aside the canvas at the door. He smiled and it was as if a bright light had been switched on or a cloud had scudded away to reveal the rays of a sun.

Phax's city remained much as it was when Rogue Avon had passed through it. The addition of Federation authority and the hungry and lascivious troops that came with it had merely secured a higher standard of living for the few who organized the black market and the gambling and prostitution rackets.

Proper villainy, however, was held in check by the brutal reputation of the occupying forces.

Bored and fractious, these supervised the mining of minimum gold and silver deposits from the mountains in the North. An activity they considered demeaning. An iron hand would be required to control the Iron Guard.

Meanwhile, the citizens played safe and went about their business, legal or otherwise, with caution.

The Prospector was known to many in the city. Despite his great height and accompanying strength, he was thought to be well meaning and harmless.

His reappearance from the wilderness provoked little reaction from his acquaintances and, thankfully, none at all from the authorities. He and the company he kept were virtually ignored.

He advised Rowena and her mother to dress plainly. Advised Rowena in particular to disguise her undoubted beauty. He gave no advice to the child. The boy had not spoken one word in his presence and, for the moment, that suited him.

Mara, together with the papers she had supplied, had revealed a stash of gold coins. The Prospector refrained from asking where she had obtained them.

Nevertheless, he accepted her gift of several pieces and used some of the remainder to grease any number of sweaty palms.

Thus it was that all four, an innocuous family, boarded the shuttle for Raphael. In the air as on the land, they excited little comment.

"One of the advantages of Federation rule," the Prospector whispered, "is that travel and communication systems function almost perfectly."

The women were too nervous to reply. The boy smiled a wan smile.

Raphael, like its satellite moon, could not be said to have changed much since Avon's visit. True, there was a more obvious military presence.

The Prospector learned from passersby, even from some soldiers, that Uranus, its satellites, its moons, everything connected with the planet, had easily and readily accepted the power of the Federation and now seemed content.

Mara and Rowena reflected bitterly on the useless suffering of both their men in the face of what seemed to be a vapid surrender to the new rule.

Although it was of no immediate concern, the Prospector also learned that the High Council was now the target of various factions determined to alter the balance of power.

Meanwhile, there was a complacency resulting from the ease with which the Federation had extended its dominion to the very edge of the Beyond, and it was inclined, for the present, to treat its border minions with a velvet glove of authority. A velvet glove that, once removed, would reveal the Iron Guard.

The outposts of Empire were well garrisoned, but the forced involved remained discreet.

The Prospector arranged their transportation to Saturn Major. "Once you get there," he warned, "if you cannot secure fresh documents, you may not proceed further. Your gold may not be sufficient to buy your security. You should seek protection."

"Protection!" Mara scoffed. "We will protect ourselves."

The Prospector shrugged. "As long as you do not constitute a threat, you are of no interest to anyone. But circumstances may change." He looked directly at the boy. The young Avon stared back at him, his dark eyes like pools of regret that held great sadness. His steady, remorseless gaze made the Prospector feel distinctly uncomfortable.

"There is nothing for me on Saturn Major," the big man said. "I will go back."

"Aren't you afraid?" Rowena asked.

"Of what? Raphael's moons can be of little use to the Federation. Unless it is assumed that they are the first line of defense against an alien invasion that may never come. I hope to be able to find a kind of peace." He looked once more at the boy. "I wish you the same."

The child smiled, but it was no longer the smile reminiscent of his father's. It was faintly ironic and, the Prospector thought, nearly forlorn.

The women were effusive in their thanks and the big man was touched when Mara tried to press more gold on him. He refused, wished them well and walked away. He did not look back.

Mara and Rowena seemed lost in thought, so the boy sat by a window of toughened crystal on the port side of the spaceship that was carrying them to Saturn Major. He stared into the inky blackness that enveloped them.

When, after some time, the ship slowed in order to

pick its route through the Rings of Saturn, he became animated, excited even, by the myriad colors through which they were passing. He watched, wide-eyed and open-mouthed, as the colors glowed, then faded. They dazzled him.

The clumsy aircraft stuttered its way into Saturn's atmosphere and its landing rockets caused mountains of dust to rise from the planet's surface. Thus, the colors of the Rings were reflected in such a way as to suggest a gigantic, silent, magical firework display.

It was with some disappointment that he left the colors behind and walked with the two women from the shuttle and into the giant terminal of the landing base that served the hi-tech city. This concourse was thronged with people of all ages, races and pigmentation.

Rowena, who had learned of it from the Prospector, made her way to a bank of video screens set against one wall of the marble-floored, steel-surrounded building. She wanted to consult the videos for information concerning accommodation, employment opportunities and local laws.

Her investigation was interrupted by a sharp, anguished cry from her son. She turned and almost cried out herself.

Her mother had collapsed to the ground and lay there, fighting for breath. The crowds had parted. Onlookers showed concern, but did nothing.

The boy was holding his grandmother's hand and she was smiling up at him. Rowena rushed over to them. Mara's breathing was faint. What little there was of it that was left to her was shallow and irregular.

Cradling Mara in her arms, Rowena looked up at the sea of faces observing them and asked for help. No one moved. She asked again, tears stinging her eyes.

At length, a man stepped forward. "There is a military hospital nearby," he said. "I'll take you there."

Mara had stopped breathing.

3

With the stranger's assistance, Rowena managed to move her mother to a monorail car that would carry them to the hospital. The man declined to travel with them.

A monorail guard kept all others at bay and radioed ahead requesting medical staff to stand by for their arrival.

Four orderlies and a doctor were waiting. They transferred Mara's seemingly lifeless body to a metal cart and wheeled her away. An attendant insisted that Rowena and the boy should wait in a small room attached to the surgery in which the doctor would conduct his examination.

The room was bright, clean and furnished with several couches covered in black hide. After a while, Rowena persuaded her son to lie down on one of them and try to sleep.

Many Earth hours passed.

With a suddenness that startled her, a communicating door slid back and a man entered.

The intruder was tall and well built. In a way, he could be described as handsome. His face was long and thin and it gave him a look of solemnity. His eyes were gray, his nose full and a little fleshy, suggesting that he might be a drinker. His hair was thick and black, highlighted with silver. His hands seemed soft and white, with long tapering fingers. He wore a green coverall of a material not unlike velvet. This was the uniform of his profession.

"I am Pi Grant," he said. "I am the chief of staff here. I am also the head surgeon." His voice was quite melodic. He had spoken very gently.

Rowena said nothing, merely stood and stared at him. The boy slept.

"Your mother is dying," the doctor went on, raising a hand as if to calm her. It was unnecessary, still she did not move. He continued, "There is nothing I can do. I'm very sorry." There was a wealth of sadness in his voice.

Rowena fought back her tears.

Pi Grant sat on the edge of the couch upon which the child was sleeping. "I wish I could have told you this terrible news more compassionately," he said, "The truth is hard to accept, even harder to convey, under any number of circumstances." He paused. "I am quite certain of diagnosis. Your mother is dying."

"Why?" Rowena's voice was barely above a whisper.

"The atmosphere has failed her. I mean, the artificial atmosphere of this planet. May I ask where she was born?"

"Miranda."

Grant nodded. "The tumbling moon."

Rowena frowned, seemed bewildered.

Pi Grant, his eyes never straying from her face, said, "It explains a great deal. Miranda is a moon of Uranus that has been falling away from its mother planet for centuries. Like a ball gathering speed as it rolls down a hill. Its atmosphere has been in a state of constant disturbance. As time has passed, it has altered radically. You understand I am putting this to you as simply as I can?"

70

Rowena nodded.

The surgeon permitted himself a deep sigh. "Anyone bred in that volatile atmosphere cannot expect to survive for long in any other. Like Saturn's, for example. This planet's artificial atmospheric umbrella is very similar to that of Earth."

"Why am I unaffected?" Rowena asked.

"I presume you were not born and bred on Miranda."

"On Raphael."

"There's the difference."

"But we lived on Phax. My mother showed no signs of deterioration there."

Grant permitted himself a slight smile. "The air on Phax could be said to be intermediate. Neither one thing, nor the other. But she would, sooner or later, have succumbed. The deterioration would have occurred suddenly, almost without warning. It was accelerated when you came here."

"Am I in danger?"

"If you mean from a similar reaction to the atmosphere," Grant said knowingly, "I'll make tests and find out."

Rowena glanced at the sleeping child and the surgeon's eyes followed her gaze. He smiled down on the boy. "I doubt that he will have a problem," he said. "The air here will suit him. He is clearly an Earth child." He looked up quickly, his gray eyes narrowing, like shafts of steel.

"That's true." Rowena said cautiously. "His father was a Federation soldier—killed in the wars for Uranus."

Grant's expression softened. "You have suffered your fair share of tragedy," he muttered, almost as if speaking to himself.

71

"May I see my mother?"

"Yes. However, she will not see you. She has entered her last sleep. She will never awaken."

Rowen could control her grief no longer. She cried out, turned her face to the wall and, as tears flooded her face, her body shook with emotion.

Grant sprang to his feet and rushed over to her. He took her in his arms, turning her towards him so that she buried her face in his chest. "We all die," he said, soothingly. "It is the only sure thing in this uncertain Universe."

Rowena looked up at him and he smoothed the tears from her cheeks. "You are in safe hands," he said.

She stepped back from his embrace and glanced across the room. Her son was sitting up on the couch and was watching them.

Grant turned. "Ah, you're awake!" he said, superfluously. He was embarrassed by the fact that he was strongly attracted to this woman and that the boy seemed aware of it.

The child's face was expressionless. Only his eyes betrayed any feeling. They were as cold as black ice.

Grant shivered involuntarily. "I'll conduct the tests I promised," he said. "It will be necessary to submit your papers to a Coordinator."

"I have gold," Rowena said suddenly.

"It would be as well not to tell anyone else that." The surgeon smiled warmly.

Rowena nodded. "I must not be separated from my son," she said forcefully.

"Consider yourselves under my personal protection," Grant said. He was aware of the boy's steady gaze and felt that he was being viewed as if under a microscope. "Shall we go?" He said weakly.

He led them through the vast surgery adjoining the

72

room in which they had waited so long for the sad news concerning Mara. Gleaming scientific equipment overlooked their progress.

"It was my decision and mine alone," Grant was saying. "I could have used drugs to keep her awake, but her breathing was too irregular and painful and her suffering would have increased by the minute. As it is, she is sedated, will sleep for some hours and pass on in peace. Pain will be but a memory. I had no choice. I hope you understand?"

Rowena nodded. She showed no hint of grief. That time was now past.

"I was called upon because I have the highest authority here," Grant continued, "with Alpha and Beta grades, that is. Anyone below can be dealt with by any of my assistants."

They walked through an open doorway into a small cubicle that contained a solitary bed and a huge vase containing artificially scented flowers.

Mara's expression as she lay asleep on the bed was one of utter contentment. A half-smile played around her lips. Her breathing was even and unhurried.

Grant stood back while Rowena, taking her mother's hands in hers, stooped to kiss her brow. Then the boy stepped forward and did likewise. The child's eyes were moist but, the surgeon noted, he did not cry as a four-year-old might be expected to do.

All three stood in the doorway for a last look at the dying woman before Rowena, quite abruptly, turned away.

Leading her child by the hand, she followed Grant to his office situated on the floor above.

This was an imposing room, luxuriously carpeted and furnished in the old style. A style once familiar on Earth, less so on Saturn Major.

The surgeon bid them be seated in comfortable chairs while he stood by a large picture window and gazed at the shimmering city outside.

"So much for death," he said quietly, "now we must deal with the living."

"The tests?" Rowena asked nervously.

He turned and smiled at her, almost lovingly. "They are very simple. A matter of taking saliva and a little blood. I'll do it now."

He walked over to a metal safe set into the wall and extracted a syringe and a number of glass phials.

He treated Rowena with great gentleness as he took the blood from her ear lobe and asked her to spit on a piece of cloth which he folded and sealed in one of the containers. Then, he placed the phials in a rack next to the safe, attached a thin wire that jutted from the wall, threw one of many switches below the rack and waited.

After a few minutes, he switched off. He walked to a computer terminal set in a corner of the room and typed in instructions. Its screen glowed, revealing a set of figures.

Grant was aware that the boy had risen, crossed the room and was standing close to him, fascinated by what he was doing.

The surgeon explained the figures. "These indicate two things," he said. "One, that you are a healthy, normal young woman. Two, that there is only a minor problem caused by entering this atmosphere. It is much as I expected. In all honesty, I have to say that your life expectancy is not as great as it would have been had you remained on Phax. On the other hand, any reduction in your life span should be minmal. Two or three Earth years at most. You are fortunate."

Federation citizens, rarely sanguine when concerned with matters of life and death under its totalitarian rule, assumed fatalism and condensed emotion. Rowena said nothing.

Grant leaned against the wall. The boy was studying the equipment.

Grant said, "It will be necessary for you to stay here for a while to acclimatize, as it were. What will you do afterwards. Where will you go?"

With Mara's imminent death, with her responsibility for the welfare of her son weighing heavily upon her, Rowena felt her strength draining away. All she could say was, "I'm not certain."

There was a very long, tense pause between them.

"I have need of a woman," Grant said at length.

Rowena looked at him sharply.

"My woman died of the Orange Plague," the man went on. "One of the legacies of the Earth Wars. Bacterial genetic weapons were used indiscriminately. There were many victims and she was one of the first. I'm talking about many years past. Long before the Federation decided on further wars for Uranus. There is no end to war, it is the humanoid vocation."

He seemed to be losing himself in his thoughts. Rowena was attentive and patient. Even the boy was listening intently.

"When all the wars concluded," Grant said, "my masters were faced with a dilemma. Many fathers were dead, maimed or maddened and all their children were alone. The Federation future must be preserved, however, and I have an adopted son and daughter. There are many men like me who have been persuaded to assist the regime in a like manner. My son is named Del, my daughter called Anna."

Grant came out of his reverie and spoke swiftly, almost nervously.

"I have much to offer in the way of position and

influence. I have some wealth and I like to think I am a fair and honorable man. As far as that is possible in this Universe. I would never abuse you or your son. I would do my best to protect you both and I would treat the boy as my own." He strode back to the window. "I realize this is very sudden." he went on. "We have known each other such a short while. I suppose I must be an impulsive man. But I think that, in this sad age, the fine moment must be seized or lost for ever." He shook his head and smiled wryly. "I'm quite shaken by all this."

Rowena walked over to him and placed a hand on his arm. "Time is a relentless enemy. You are merely trying to defeat it."

Grant took her in his arms and looked into her eyes. "Are you prepared to accept my extraordinary offer?"

"All the benefits would be on my side." Rowena said. "All I can do is promise to try and alleviate any pain you may suffer. Be a companion in your loneliness."

"From the moment I saw you, I needed you. Do you believe me?"

Rowena looked to the boy who was leaning against the wall and watching them intently. "The Federation could be hell for us," she said. "We need your protection."

"You have it." Grant said with finality.

Rowena smiled brightly. "I accept!"

The surgeon smiled back at her, his glance tender and approving. "What is the boy's name?"

Rowena's smile faded. "He is called Kerguelen." She looked at her son. "It means 'desolation'!"

4

Within nine Earth days, Rowena and the boy were ensconced in Grant's palatial mansion situated in the protected Alpha grade suburbs.

They quickly learned that their benefactor was richer, more powerful and had greater influence than they had been led to believe.

His great house was filled with fabulous carpets from the weavers of Alpha Centauri. The walls of the vast reception rooms were hung with famous paintings from World and Venusian masters. Furniture was of rich mahogany and a teak as tough as that of Raphael, but far more decorative.

There were many servants. Slaves from Neptune, from the moon called Titan and from any number of Jupiter's inhabited satellites.

Del and Anna Grant were natural brother and sister. They were the children of a Federation commander, a close friend of Pi Grant, who had been killed in action on the very globe where Mara had been born—the tumbling moon, Miranda.

Rowena and Kerguelen were welcomed enthusiastically. Pampered and fussed over, it seemed that their hosts' love and respect knew no bounds.

All mourned at Mara's funeral. The body was burned and the ashes fired into the colored Rings of Saturn.

Rowena, touched by the affection and generosity of the Grant family and household, swiftly set about establishing herself within it.

Del Grant was grown to ten Earth years and Anna

was but a few months senior to Rowena's son.

A slight, pretty girl, Anna easily adapted to her role of sister and protector of Kerguelen. She grew to love the boy and, sometime later, the grown man.

Pi Grant bonded formally with Rowena and, according to the custom, adopted her child.

Kerguelen, a difficult name for the servants and children, was foreshortened. For the time being, Rogue Avon's son was to be called Kerr Grant.

None of these happenings were extraordinary in the Federation society of that time and place.

Continuous warfare had decimated the populations of the nine planets and vast areas that had once supported wild, humanoid, even alien life had been devastated by the pollution, destruction and decay that attends the beast called Man.

It was, therefore, quite natural for Pi Grant to seek a mother for his adopted children and a companion for his bed. The established order required, even commanded, continuity and rationalization.

He was envied by many. Rowena, though not an intellectual equal, was possessed of beauty and a comparable charm. The general female population of Saturn Major tended to be devoid of both.

Even the fact that her father had been a dissident in the wars for Uranus hardly raised an eyebrow. Those wars were long gone and there was a new attitude in the corridors of power that led to the chamber housing the Federation High Council. An attitude of compromise and conciliation. This was a time for the ambitious to catch their breath, to watch and wait.

In any case, the daughter of a little known deceased rebel posed no threat and Grant's influence was enough to squash any rumor or criticism.

Mara's precious papers, as far as they went, had

sufficed to satisfy an investigation by the Coordinator. The only thing that puzzled, intrigued him, was the boy's origin.

Rowena, sensing danger, claimed that she had never known his father beyond one brief encounter. She claimed Kerguelen was a child of rape. That ended the matter.

Grant laughed at her when she offered him the gold bequeathed her by her mother.

"I have no need of it," he said. "In you, I have something more precious than gold."

On their bonding night, he took her very gently through their act of love. It was as if he was handling a rare and delicate object that might break.

She was unskilled in the practice of sex but, contrary to her imaginings, this pleased rather than deterred him. He delighted in her and in her magnificent, sensuous young body. His lovemaking was tender and considerate. A severe contrast to the almost violent coupling she had experienced with Rogue Avon.

In truth, she felt she was a poor reward for Grant's generosity, care and undoubted love. Nonetheless, she appreciated the power that she had now achieved over him.

Now she began to taste the sweet corruption that the Federation system offered its privileged grades. As long as she continued to please her man, appeared witty, charming and reasonably intelligent and as long as she flattered and subtly insinuated herself in the affections of Grant's influential colleagues and friends, she would herself achieve influence and the tools of deceit.

Faithful in her fashion to both Pi Grant and her new Federation masters and accepted as a member of Saturn Major society at its highest level, she set about her twin tasks.

Using all the facilities that the system and privilege could provide, she would raise her son to manhood. At no time would she permit him to become anyone's creature but her own.

She would seek any and all information concerning Rogue Avon. If, as she suspected and as he himself had suggested, he had been hunted and killed by his enemies, then she would discover the manner of his death. For the moment, this was her main concern. Later, her vengeance would become her grand obsession.

She set about learning all she could of the workings of the regime she had once been taught to hate. Her hatred now tempered by opportunism.

Since the internecine wars on Earth and its neighboring planets, there had been many rearrangements of the Federation power structure.

The population had shrunk alarmingly. Only now, by encouragement, sometimes through force, was it on the increase. Soon, the Federation would be on the march again. It would search for the living space to replace that devastation caused by the lost ambitions of forgotten families and factions.

For the time being, the Alpha and Beta grades indulged in almost barbarous hedonism but, all the while, they recruited and reserved their strength.

The grades below were drugged into submission. They performed the menial tasks and provided the cannon fodder for future adventures.

Strangely, these underprivileged masses learned to admire their place in the scheme of Federation affairs. History and the men who mould it have often succeeded in creating such a class. Propaganda, fear, controlled pleasure and war are near perfect instruments for nurturing a slave mentality.

Inevitably, there were aberrants. These were silenced

by law, by torture or by death.

Death had brought Rowena and Pi Grant together. It was the only thing that would separate them and it would come sooner rather than later.

Meanwhile, there was life. Rowena, determined to live it to the full, never ignored what she considered her duty towards her new family and she made every effort to control her son's destiny.

She enrolled him in the military college that was fast gaining a reputation for excellence throughout the known Universe. It was the college where Pruth had once taught.

Kerr revealed an aptitude for languages and a love of mathematics.

The first skill surprised many, for he was considered a taciturn youth. The second, presumably, was a legacy from Rogue Avon's defeated father. A gift from a lost generation that was useful in two essential fields—finance and gunnery.

It was the tradition that each student be partnered throughout his school life by a "Brother." Kerr was linked with Amiyak, a fair-haired, studious boy who was the adopted son of Makarov, the Principal of the Academy. Amiyak's rheumy eyes put Rowena in mind of a sad dog.

Kerr began to wonder if there were any natural sons in the Federation. There were, but they were considered the backbone of Empire and were housed and schooled on Earth.

Although there is no greater enmity than that between members of the same family who have fallen out, blood was still considered a stronger indication of allegiance than anything else. In time, Kerr Avon, known as Grant, would unravel that paradox.

With the quiescence of peace and the momentarily

stagnant ambition of his Federation benefactors, he was permitted a life of luxury and contentment. He learned from the best teachers and used the best equipment that Pi Grant could provide. He was being groomed, as were all the others, to be a part of the officer elite that would lead the Iron Guards and Death Squads in the future building of Empire.

It soon became apparent that he and Amiyak were of above-average intelligence. Amiyak, despite his quiet dedication to the learning process, despite his slight frame, was gaining strength and would grow into a hardened adult. Kerr, on the other hand, preferred guile to force, always ensuring that any opponent was in a weak position and on unfamiliar ground before he struck.

Thus it was that the two of them gained the respect of their tutors and fellow students alike. A respect that made them candidates for advancement. The rumors abounded that they would achieve the ultimate and be entitled to complete their education on Earth, the breeding ground for the regime's true elite.

This delighted Rowena and she watched her son grow with evident satisfaction. She shared his happiness with his academic successes. Admired his cunning and ruthlessness in combat examinations. She taught him to be self-contained and to trust only a few.

That she succeeded in moulding him in the image she required was evidenced by the fact that, apart from his "Brotherly," relationship with Amiyak and an obvious affection for Anna, he formed no close connection with any other. Rowena remained the strongest influence on him.

When a combat instructor described him as vicious, amoral and a crude opportunist, Pi Grant wondered if it was a rebuke. His mother considered it a compliment and an indication of the realization of her intent.

The boy grew to resemble his natural father.

In almost every geture, in his deceptive movements, in his quick brain, in his still menace he reminded Rowena of that time long ago on Phax when she had been loved by a man she would never see again. Except, perhaps, reborn in their son.

It was about the eyes that he most resembled Rogue Avon. His were the same dark pools of pain and disappointment, alleviated only by the bright smile that was all too rare.

When he had attained fifteen Earth years and had been a "Grant" for little more than ten of them, she knew the time was right to tell him the truth about his father. For, by this time, she had learned it herself.

5

To all intents and purposes, Rowena had been for ten years a dutiful, beautiful, devoted mother and, for want of a better word, wife.

However, as she grew older and acquired the knowledge and accompanying cynicism of maturity, a canker grew within her that would lead to her ultimate destruction.

With all the guile that could be described as the most useful attribute of her sex, she gleaned information from Grant, his colleague the Coordinator and others that led her to a full understanding of the philosophy of the Federation, its politics and of the struggling factions within it. She learned most from Amiyak's adoptive father, the Principal of the Academy—Makarov.

Confined to a wheelchair, he was a thin, angular, cantankerous, garrulous relic from a bygone age. Of indeterminate age, he was certainly old enough to be not long for this Universe.

Ambitious for power, he had formed an alliance with a number of other Federation luminaries and tried to force himself on to the High Council. He made no bones about the fact that he had felt himself betrayed when his friends had switched allegiance and he had been dispatched to Saturn, far from the heartbeat of the system he had sought to influence.

He had revealed his knowledge of Rogue Avon and the circumstance surrounding his death.

It was at a dinner party. A glittering Saturn evening arranged to celebrate Rowena and Pi Grant's bonding. Markarov was an honored guest and he spoke the name that seared into Rowena's brain like a lightning bolt.

Try as she might, she could not find a way to persuade the old man to elaborate on his brief overheard remark.

She encouraged Grant to invite the Principal to their mansion whenever the opportunity arose. Sooner or later she would extract what information she could from him.

Meanwhile, her enquiries, of necessity discreet, produced nothing. There was no record of Rogue Avon's existence. It was as if he had never been.

Makarov, flattered by the attention of Grant's much-admired lady, was a frequent visitor and, slowly, he revealed snippets of information that, in time, Rowena was able to piece together into a cogent whole.

She learned the names of his former "allies," Axel Reiss, Pel Gros and a Martian called Pruth. Information about the latter was easily obtained.

"I've never seen a Martian," Rowena said, as she and

the old man sat in a glass-covered conservatory attached to Grant's house.

"You haven't missed much," he replied irritably.

"What was he like?" She smiled and the question seemed innocent enough.

The old man snarled and flecks of saliva danced on his withered lips. "An intellectual who became a buffoon. He was seduced by his ambition and greed."

Rowena plied Makarov with the best Saturn wine she could find in Grant's cellar. "What happened to him?"

"He conceived some outlandish plan that he hoped would frighten the High Council so that he could assume the role of a savior. So that we all could, for that matter. I was against it from the start, but Axel, once he became aware of it, was enthusiastic. Unusual, I thought. Axel is a cautious man."

"What was the plan?"

The man smiled evilly. "You're too young to remember the wars," he said patronizingly. "The High Council was split. Not to put too fine a point on it, the majority were terrified."

"It's hard to imagine the Federation would be terrified of anything." Rowena said quietly.

"Well, it all started to go wrong when the dissidents on Uranus put up a better fight than expected. That's when we saw our chance. Our chance to gain influence, to discipline the Federation philosophy, to create a strong, unbeatable war machine that could even enter the Beyond and conquer galaxies that haven't yet been thought of, let alone discovered."

"Why?"

"Why not?"

Rowena smiled. "But you failed?"

Makarov grimaced. "Pruth failed. Axel had to pick up the pieces."

"Pruth was killed?"

"Yes. His grand strategy backfired on him." The Principal laughed. "Almost literally backfired."

Rowena said nothing, merely waited for him to continue in his own time.

"Why do you want to know all this?" he asked suddenly.

"I'm surprised that a man of your undoubted ability has not been more greatly honored by the system. I want to know why."

The old man snickered appreciatively. "They could have had my head, but they didn't. I'm indebted to Axel for that."

"He sounds an interesting man."

"He's the most ruthless, cruel, savage, brilliant man I have ever met. Without him, and men like him, we would be ruled by aliens or homosexual weaklings."

"Perhaps I'll meet him one day?"

Makarov grinned lasciviously. "I'd like to be there when you do."

Very gently, very subtly, Rowena led him back to the continuation of the story she wanted to hear. "What was the plan?" she asked when she thought the moment was appropriate. "You still haven't told me Pruth's plan."

"Well, I've already told you that some of the Council were panicking. Of course, the Iron Guard soon destroyed any opposition on Uranus, but the fact that they were needed, our best troops to quell a bunch of ill-equipped guerrillas, was alarming. Pruth wanted to prey on that alarm, to exacerbate it. As luck would have it, he came into contact with a fugitive, one with a heavy price on his head. At first he was inclined to collect the reward but, after making enquiries, he took a different course."

Rowena grew impatient. The old man stopped talking, seemed lost in thought.

"What did his enquiries reveal?" she prompted.

"What? Oh, his name, his reputation. The fugitive had achieved some fame when he deserted the Federation. You could say that he had been a footnote in our history books."

"What was his name?" Rowena was almost breathless with the anticipation of hearing it again.

"Rogue Avon. Not much of a man, but a man for all that. He certainly shook us up. We manipulated him. Made him run for Earth. He was going there anyway, we helped him on his way. We wanted to show the Council that one man, if he was determined enough, could penetrate any defense they could devise. Pruth was meant to take him alive, but Avon outmaneuvered him. It was left to Axel to finish him off."

The Principal did not seem to notice Rowena's sharp intake of breath.

"Anyway," he continued, "Pruth was dead and we had been made to look incompetent. Axel salvaged something, I suppose, but he sacrificed me in the process."

"You did say he was a cruel man."

Makarov laughed. "I did, didn't I? What I couldn't understand, still can't, is why Axel went along with it. We were like children trying to gain the attention and the admiration of grownups. Not his style at all."

"But if your men had been shown to be the only ones who could capture Rogue Avon, a man your propaganda had built into a great threat, then surely it would have served your purpose?"

Makarov sighed wearily. "That was the trouble. We could have taken him, should have taken him, at any time. We let him run too far and too fast."

"How did he die?"

"Pruth?"

"No."

"Axel cut him to pieces. They fought man on man. I got the feeling it was very personal."

"Why?" Rowena was hanging on his every word.

"I've no idea."

Later, during the course of further conversations with the aging Principal, Rowena learned the details of Avon's run to Earth. Of how he had killed a villain named Gilpin. Of how he had outgunned Pruth. Of how Axel Reiss had cut his head off with a twin-bladed knife with serrated edge.

It was then that the tumor of revenge lodged in her heart. Makarov, Pel Gros, Alex Reiss would die by her hand, or by that of Rogue Avon's son, or they would both die in the attempt.

Makarov's demise was easily contrived.

On an evening when she had arranged for him to dine with her and Pi Grant, she placed a fierce, slow-acting poison in the wine that he was accustomed to consume to excess.

He took ten days to die. As the final agony came upon him, Rowena leaned across his death bed and whispered one word in his ear. The old man's eyes opened with shock and surprise. The word "Avon" was the last he ever heard. Rowena's triumphant, cruel smile the last thing he ever saw.

6

Rowena was impatient to continue, to conclude her vengeance, but her remaining targets were inaccessible.

Pel Gros was a member of the High Council—someone who had succeeded where Makarov had failed—and controlled a huge business enterprise from Earth. Axel Reiss was an unknown quanitity. Officially an adviser on military matters, in this time of comparative peace, he was keeping a low, almost invisible, profile.

It was a Federation law that, unless he had been born there or was of proven Earth blood, no citizen could visit the mother planet of Empire. The World was racially pure. It was a fortress protecting the values for which the Federation stood and on which its survival depended.

The hint that Kerr might conclude his education on Earth soon proved to be more than that. He was officially ordered to enter the Iron School.

Situated in the lush mid-Western section of the World, it was the best, the only school for ambitious, talented students.

Rowena found it hard to contain herself. Her plan was being carried out by the Federation itself. Her only regret was that she could not accompany her son on their trail of destruction.

She worried that the task that now lay upon the boy would prove too onerous. She need not have concerned herself.

Mother and son strolled through an orchard designed

and carefully nurtured by Pi Grant. Artificial birdsong filled the air. No real birds sing on Saturn.

"I don't have to tell you how proud I am," Rowena said.

Young Avon, who was now fifteen Earth years, said nothing.

"You are being given every opportunity," his mother continued. "A fine education, a settled, secure environment."

"And a parallel education from you."

Rowena smiled at the interjection. "I trust you will put it to good use."

Avon shrugged.

Rowena, detecting an air of rebellion in the sullen youth, said, "Never forget, never forgive. Promise me that!"

Avon's sad, dark eyes scrutinized her carefully. "Tell me why?" he asked.

She took him by the shoulders and held him like a lover. "They killed your father and they must pay. They toyed with him, hunted him down like an animal, and then they destroyed him."

"We all have to die," her son whispered.

Rowena held him away from her and looked into the familiar eyes that haunted her with memories. "I have nothing else to live for," she said. "There isn't anything else in the Universe that I can bring myself to care about."

Kerr Avon shrugged himself free of her grasp. "I could contradict you," he said, an ironic smile playing at the corners of his mouth, "but I won't."

They walked on through the aisle of fruit trees, a breeze ruffling their clothing and hair.

"There's no purpose to life," Avon said. "It's just a tiresome journey towards death. I rather wish I had never been born."

Rowena was momentarily stunned by the remark. "You have one important purpose," she said finally.

Her son treated her to a rare, dazzling smile. "For the second time I ask you—why?"

"You remind me so much of him," Rowena said, striving to contain her emotion.

"But I'm not him and I never will be. Oh, I'll complete the task you have set me. I'll be the instrument of your terrible revenge!" he laughed. "I'll kill Gros and Reiss for you. Then what?"

Rowena said nothing. There was nothing she could say.

Avon listened to the non-existent birds. "I have no hatred for the Federation," he said. "I am indifferent. Of course, I will try to avoid the pain it is capable of inflicting and I'll enjoy the privileges I am afforded. What I would really prefer. . ." He hesitated. "I would prefer to be alone. It's a kind of hell to be a part of the human race."

Rowena felt anger welling up inside her. "As long as Grant lives," she said, "I can have everything the Federation has to offer. So can you. When he dies, his protection dies with him. Don't imagine that we have no enemies. Envy of success and wealth ensure that we have many. It's possible that your true identity will be discovered and that knowledge may be used against us. It's a regrettable trait of Earthlings that, the higher you go, the greater the number of those who desire to bring you down."

"I very much doubt that the sins of my father will be visited on me," Avon said quietly. "I have too much to offer our Federation overlords. Remember, I'm not only your child, but also a child of the regime. Besides, Makarov was right. Rogue Avon does not feature largely in the Federation memory. He couldn't cope with the system, so the system destroyed him. It seems logical."

"I won't rest until Reiss and Pel Gros have paid my price," Rowena said fiercely.

Avon eyed her coolly. "Mother—I think you are quite mad!"

She struck him a stinging blow across the face. He stepped back, his eyes narrowing, his stance tight with menace.

The moment passed quickly, but Rowena, recognizing her vulnerability to his anger, made no move towards her son. Instead, he came to her.

"I'm sorry," he said, but she wasn't sure if he meant it. Then he smiled. "You may count the Earth days that Reiss and Pel Gross have left. But you must understand that I don't consider I owe you anything. I make a present to you of their deaths." He walked away from her and leaned against an apple tree. The leaves of its branches shadowed his face. "When it's all over," he continued, "I don't expect I'll ever see you again."

Rowena turned away, tears in her eyes. When she looked back, Avon had gone. Only the breeze remained.

7

Del Grant had been sent to the Iron School some years before. Neither Rowena nor Avon had known him well. Rowena because she was obsessed with her natural son, Avon because he was so much younger than his adoptive brother. By the time he had achieved an age when any kind of friendship might have developed, Del was gone.

There remained Anna.

For the ten years that they had been together, an affection had grown between the quiet, observant young boy and the ebullient wisp of a girl.

They had shared the pains of growing up, such as they were. Their time together, limited because of Avon's forced attendance at the military college, was precious. Truth to tell, Kerr was in love with her and it seemed she returned the favor.

When the time came for him to travel to Earth, a kind of gloom settled on the Grant household.

During the course of his last night on Saturn, Anna visited him in his room. An ominous silence enveloped the rest of the house.

It was Avon's custom to lie naked on his bed. Anna wore a simple, silk nightgown. She looked down on him.

"I won't see you for a long time," she said.

"No." He was unperturbed by the steadiness of her gaze.

"I'll be a grown woman when we meet again."

He smiled. "You're a grown woman now."

There was a long silence.

"I'd like you to prove it to me," she said.

Avon sat up. "Why?"

She laughed a bubbling, infectious laugh. "That's your favorite word."

"But the question is never answered."

Anna removed her gown.

Avon calmly appraised her nude body. Slightly built, she had a round, pretty face. Her nose was endearingly askew, her mouth full and mockingly sensual. Her long fair hair partly obscured her gray eyes. Her complexion rivalled that of the skin of a peach. Her breasts were small and firm, their nipples crimson and erect.

He pulled her down beside him on the bed.

Slowly and tenderly, they carassed each other, searched each other's bodies with hands and mouths. When he felt the time was right, Avon entered her with a sudden, violent movement that caused her to cry out. Her breathing became rapid. She felt the exhilerating combination of pain and pleasure. Pinning her beneath him so that she could hardly move, Avon thrust deep within her and smothered her mouth with a kiss that stifled her scream as she climaxed. Bathed in perspiration, they held each other and loved each other until the grim light of the Saturn dawn forced them apart.

Avon slept.

When he awoke, it was to discover that Anna had left him and returned to her own room.

He lay there, silent and thoughtful until the time came for him to prepare himself for the journey to Earth.

When he was ready, Rowena accompanied him to the space terminal where a Starship awaited him and Amiyak. His "Brother" was already aboard.

Pi Grant, to his displeasure, had been called away. Something at the military hospital, he had been informed, required his urgent attention.

While the technicians prepared the ship for flight, Avon and his mother stood apart.

They looked at each other, then Avon took Rowena in his arms and kissed her lightly on the lips. "I'll try to live up to your expectations," he said.

She whispered, "Good luck!"

Avon smiled broadly. "Luck will have nothing to do with it!"

She watched him as he strode away and mounted the steps of the spacecraft. He turned for one last glance at her before disappearing into its flight deck.

Rowena sighed deeply. She did not wait for the ship's takeoff, but slowly walked away.

When she returned to the mansion, the Saturn Coordinator was waiting for her. His name was Sabbath.

She ushered him into the conservatory where Makarov had been so well entertained. Where Rowena had murdered him.

The Coordinator was a comparative stranger. She had known him only briefly when he investigated her background.

Sabbath was a short, stocky man. His cold, watery blue eyes gleamed at her from folds of pitted skin. He was quite bald. He smiled, his thick lips curling back over discolored teeth. "So! He's gone!"

Rowena offered him a drink which he declined with an almost imperceptible shake of his head. His eyes never left her.

Rowena forced a smile. "To what do I owe this pleasure?" she asked.

Sabbath returned her smile. "It is my pleasure, not yours."

"What do you mean?"

"I think you know." Sabbath rose to his feet and stood directly in front of her.

Rowena sat looking up at him, tense and silent.

The Coordinator began to pace to and fro. "Why didn't you tell me long ago that your son is the son of a traitor?"

She controlled herself admirably. "Would it have made any difference if I had?"

Sabbath laughed, a dry sinister sound.

"In any case," Rowena went on, "who are you that I should have to justify myself to you? Perhaps you have forgotten that I am Grant's woman? Overlooked his power!"

"He has no power," Sabbath spoke so quietly that she hardly heard him.

Rowena tried to take control of the situation. "You have discovered that Kerr is Rogue Avon's son. I say again, what difference does it make?"

"Rogue Avon is dead."

"I know. He was killed on Earth by a man named Axel Reiss."

Sabbath looked at her sharply.

"The boy is of the Federation," Rowena continued, "you should be in no doubt of that."

The Coordinator tossed his head disparagingly. "If there was a doubt, he would be dead by now."

"Then, what would seem to be the problem?" she asked, smiling sweetly.

"You were a traitor's slut." Sabbath spoke venemously.

Rowena stood up and walked over to him. Without warning, she slapped him hard across the face with the back of her hand. Sabbath reeled away from the blow. He shrank against a wall, licking flecks of blood from his lips.

"How long have you known about my son?" Rowena asked as if nothing had happened.

The Coordinator's eyes gleamed malevolently. "Long enough. It was a matter of little importance until Makarov died. He had mentioned to me in passing that you had been questioning him about Rogue Avon. I think you killed Makarov."

Rowena smiled serenely. "I think you will find that rather difficult to prove."

Sabbath grinned. "Be sure your sins will find you out," he said.

"Well, you appear to have cast the first stone and

nissed!"

This time he laughed. "You're a formidable woman."

"What now?" Rowena asked as she walked back to her chair.

"The matter has been taken out of my hands. I was given orders to put certain questions to you."

"By whom?"

"Axel Reiss."

Rowena sighed. "That name again. Why is the fact that I bore Rogue Avon's son so important? What was there about Rogue that can matter so much so long after his death?"

Sabbath wiped the blood from his mouth and leaned nonchalantly against the wall. "He was a rebel. Very impressive. A guerrilla who scared the pants off certain members of the High Council. They've put them back on and they don't want to risk losing them again."

Rowena laughed. "I'm sworn to kill Axel Reiss," she said finally.

"I'm sure he's aware of that."

She gave him a searching look. "So, he knows that Kerr is Rogue's son?"

"There's very little he doesn't know."

"I would like to meet him."

"I expect you will. In hell—if there is such a place."

"Our son would say that there is," she replied sadly. "I still don't understand what you expect of me?"

Sabbath's face was a mask.

She smiled at him beguilingly. "Won't you tell me?"

He looked solemn. "I've been sent to kill you."

"Is that all? I thought you had some questions?"

He looked at her, admiring her apparent imperturbability. "Grant has known the boy's identity for some time. Not that it matters, he's already being persuaded to hold his tongue. After all, he has children who can

97

be used as levers on his conscience."

Rowena, outwardly calm, was shaken. "What about your questions?"

"Reiss wants to know if Rogue Avon ever mentioned his name."

"Why should he have?"

Sabbath seemed genuinely surprised. "You don' know?"

"What don't I know?"

A sudden noise distracted them. The door to the main house slid back and Grant entered. He looked much older, sadder, as if he had suffered a terrible defeat.

Rowena ran to his side, took hold of him and led him to a chair. "What's wrong?"

Grant looked up at her. "There's an authority greater then mine," he said. "I must lose you to it."

Rowena knelt beside him. "Axel Reiss?"

Grant nodded.

"You would think he was the devil himself," Rowena said bitterly.

Sabbath whispered. "He could very well be."

Grant buried his head in his hands. "There is nothing I can do," he said.

For a brief moment, Rowena despised him. She stood. "What are you?" she said. "I've lived with you for ten years and I don't know."

"He's a creature of the Federation," Sabbath said. "He owes it a greater allegiance than he owes you. He'll sacrifice you to it."

"Will you?" Rowena asked.

Grant got slowly to his feet. "I've protected, loved you even, for ten years," he said. "Now I am a dead man and my protection dies with me."

Rowena's worst fears were about to be realized.

98

"Why?" she asked.

Sabbath said, "The house is surrounded by a detachment of Subsidiaries. All your slaves are dead. Now it's your turn."

Rowena rounded on him. "But why?"

The Coordinator shrugged. "This is the way Reiss wants it. Grant can go on living if he will. He has something to offer." He flicked a glance at the still, silent, gray-faced man. "The decision is his."

The tall windows of the conservatory shattered. Shards of glass littered the floor.

Rowena sprang back in alarm, Grant fell back against a door. Sabbath had not moved a muscle.

"Some of my Subsidiaries are getting impatient," he said. He looked at Grant. "Walk out now," he commanded.

Grant hesitated, glanced at Rowena, then walked to the windows, his feet crunching glass. A burst from a pump action caught him full in the chest and hurled him back into the room.

Rowena cried out with terror as Sabbath sprang at her and knocked her to the ground. Like a jackal savaging a dying animal, he tore off her clothing. She fought him like a tiger. she scratched his face and gouged his eyes. She kicked and struggled. But he had great strength and, at the last, she could not resist him.

After a while, he stood. Rowena, cut and bruised and bleeding, lay whimpering at his feet. He turned on his heel and, without a backward glance, walked through the gap left by the shattered window frame into Grant's orchard.

Rowena, shrinking in horror from Grant's bloody corpse, tried desperately to control the fear that gripped every fiber of her being. A strange, gurgling sound made her look up.

Anna Grant, a wild look in her eyes, her knuckles jammed into her mouth to stifle hysterical laughter, was clinging to a heavy curtain draped by the side of the window frame. Her face was flushed with excitement. Her whole body trembled in a kind of ecstasy.

Rowena, frightened and bewildered, snarled her disgust. But, before she could bring herself to speak, a shadow fell across her as a man entered the room.

She held back a cry of recognition. The intruder was not Rogue Avon, but bore an uncanny resemblance to him, as if he were a mirror image. The man smiled and any resemblance ended. "I am Axel Reiss," he said coldly, "I understand you would like to kill me?"

Anna Grant giggled uncontrollably.

Reiss turned to her. "Get out!" He said.

She pouted at him.

Reiss spoke very softly to her. "I won't tell you again. You can wait for me."

Anna smiled, first at him, then at Rowena. When she was certain that Reiss's attention had reverted to the other woman, she walked out.

There was a terrible silence.

Reiss knelt down and looked into Rowena's eyes. "He never mentioned my name?"

She shook her head and looked away from him.

He touched her face with his fingertips, then he stood and followed Anna outside.

Rowena, rigid with fear, moaned softly to herself.

The Subsidiaries came to her and, when they were finished with her, she was dead.

There was no sound. Even the artificial birdsong had been silenced.

PART THREE

Axel Reiss

1

By the time a Death Squad gun ship arrived to collect him, Reiss was shivering in the intense cold. In company with Rogue Avon's corpse, he was covered in a light dusting of snow.

He tossed a cloth bundle into the hold of the aircraft before climbing into the cockpit beside the pilot. "You took your time!" he said, but in a neutral tone.

The pilot shrugged and activated the controls. Noise from the engine defeated further conversation.

Reiss was flown to the mountain fortress called Lupus. This was protected by heavy laser guns and invisible airborne mines, and was garrisoned by the very best and most trustworthy Iron Guards.

It was here, in an old but luxuriously appointed castle, that the High Council of the Federation on Earth held court.

After allowing himself a few hours to prepare

himself, Reiss, accompanied by Pel Gros and Makarov, entered the chamber where the two most powerful beings in the then Universe awaited him.

The room was enormous. On three sides were high windows that afforded spectacular views of the surrounding snow-capped mountains. On the fourth side was a plain wall upon which was hung a masterpiece that had survived over a thousand years. It had been painted by someone called Bosch and depicted a version of hell that Reiss considered particularly apt.

Beneath the art work, set out approximately three meters from the wall, stood a long, richly ornamented desk. Behind this were two armchairs padded with velvet. In front were two plain wooden chairs. Reiss and Gros occupied these latter. Makarov was in his wheelchair.

Facing them across the desk sat a slim, effete albino known as Blanca. Next to him was a tall, graceful woman. She was dressed entirely in emerald green silk. Her red hair and scarlet painted lips provided vivid contrast. She was called Vasht and it was she who spoke first.

"I trust this enquiry will not take too long?" Her voice was deep and attractive, her tone authoritative. She was not a woman to be taken lightly.

Pel Gros, a sleek, well-fleshed diplomat who, in Reiss's eyes, strongly resembled a mole, replied. "Surely, there is no need for an enquiry?"

"I will be the judge of that," Vasht said icily.

Gros nodded his acquiescence.

Reiss said, "I will speak for all three of us."

The albino, Blanca, yawned, swivelled his chair away from them and gazed out of one of the tall windows. He seemed uninterested in the proceedings.

"Very well," Vasht said. "You may begin."

Reiss stood up, placed the bundle of cloth he had brought with him from Rogue Avon's killing ground on the desk in front of her and returned to his seat.

"That contains the rebel's head," he said quietly.

Vasht didn't bat an eyelid. Neither did she attempt to examine the bundle.

"There is no more certain proof of a man's death." Reiss continued.

Vasht extracted a long, thin cigar from a jewelled box and lit it with a gold lighter encrusted with diamonds. She inhaled deeply and expelled smoke in Reiss's direction.

He smiled his cold smile. "Any threat posed by this—how shall I call him?—this 'terrorist,' is now removed. He was a tough opponent. You were well advised to fear him."

"Should we now fear you?" Vasht asked.

"That is for you to decide."

The woman frowned. Makarov attempted to speak, but she silenced him with a gesture. The rings she wore on every finger of each hand sparkled in the light of the brilliant sun outside. "You assured us," she said, "that all resistance was at an end. That the wars for Uranus had been concluded and that the Federation faced no further opposition. Except, perhaps, from aliens who inhabit the Beyond!"

"The truth."

"A half truth!"

"As you will."

"We learned, to our consternation," Vasht went on, "that the Martian had devised an elaborate plan so that we might be embarrassed by the ease with which one man, alone in the Universe, could threaten us." She spoke quietly, no hint of anger in her voice.

Reiss cleared his throat. "It was a good plan, but it

got a little out of hand. Martians do tend to underestimate those of us who are of the Earth."

Vasht smiled and clouds of smoke issued from her mouth.

Reiss eyed her mischievously. "However, the plan could be said to have worked to your advantage."

Vasht looked to her companion as the albino swung his attention back to the assembled company.

"Of course," she said, an equally mischievous glint in her eye, "Blanca was a little upset when Pruth met his untimely end."

Blanca's pale pink eyes fixed themselves on Reiss. "The Martian's death could have been avoided," he said. His speech was sibilant. He hissed his consonants. This form of address and the fact that he never blinked resulted in his often being referred to, but never to his face, as the White Cobra.

Reiss studied him thoughtfully. "We must all pay for our mistakes," he said at length.

Blanca attempted a wry smile. "Pruth paid a little too heavily for my liking."

Vasht placed a bejewelled hand on his arm. "We all know how fond you were of the Martian," she said. "You should be grateful to Reiss that he has avenged his death."

Blanca looked at her sharply. She smiled seductively and, after a moment, he appeared mollified. With a sigh, he swung his chair away and resumed his pose of indifference. But there was little doubt that he listened intently to the conversation that followed.

Reiss, aware of his and speaking mainly for Blanca's benefit, said, "Pruth was profiting from the hunting down of fugitives with a price on their heads. He wanted to prove that he could deliver one of the most dangerous to Earth's doorstep. Avon outwitted him.

You went along with the scheme because it was a way of illustrating to the Council our vulnerability to the determined aggression of one man. The point was proved. Any danger to the Federation can be faced and eliminated. Except. . ." He paused for effect.

"Except that one man, or a small group of men, will cause greater problems than a host of aliens. It is a symptom of our time. All over the Universe we are seeing evidence that supports the possibility. The Council was smug and complacent. Fat with power, impotent through greed and sloth. In this new era, such complacency must be avoided. Sometime in the future, there will be a banding together of determined individuals who will attempt to blow us apart. Rogue Avon, perhaps, was the first of the few who could do it. We must be prepared for those who will follow."

There was a silence during which Vasht crushed out her cigar in a gold receptacle. "I had no idea you had such a talent for passionate oratory," she said drily.

Blanca sniggered.

Gros and Makarov sat still and straight, conscious of the tension in the room.

Reiss shrugged and lounged in his chair.

Vasht spoke quietly and calmly. "We accept all you have said. Blanca and I, at your prompting, have succeeded, if only temporarily, in removing the dross that sat with us from the High Council. We have taken note of your warnings and will anticipate and strangle at birth any opposition to our rule." She smiled. "I mean, of course, opposition to Federation rule."

"That's easier said than done," Reiss replied coolly.

"We can but try." Vasht sighed.

Blanca spoke once more. "There remains one other matter," he said, malevolence matched with curiosity in his tone. "It occurs to me that there is more to this business with Rogue Avon than meets the eye."

Everyone's attention concentrated on Reiss.

Avon's half-brother smiled and it was as if a cloud had smothered the sun and the temperature had dropped several degrees. "As far as I am concerned," he said, "this wasn't business. It was strictly personal!"

2

Vasht and Blanca co-opted Pel Gros onto the High Council. Makarov, whom neither fully trusted, was offered and dared not refuse the control of the military on Saturn. Neither Gros nor Reiss seemed prepared to speak up for him and support his bid for a higher position.

The cripple spoke bitterly to Reiss. "Why should Gros be puffed up, while I am exiled to the far regions?"

Reiss attempted to placate him. "You will be our eyes and ears on Saturn. Our early warning system for when the trouble begins. As it surely will."

"You promised me better than this."

Reiss rounded on him. "Vasht despises you. Worse, she fears you. Your influence with the army has not been overlooked. It was stupid of you to assume that, once she achieved power, she could bring herself to trust you."

Makarov struck his hands against the wheels of his chair. "I was crippled in the wars she fought against the old regime. Long before the wars for Uranus raised her so high. I deserve more than she deigns to offer."

Reiss sighed. "She could have you killed. With Gros on the Council, with me behind you, she won't dare.

Be thankful for small mercies."

"I feel betrayed," Makarov whined.

Reiss knelt beside the wheelchair and looked into his eyes. "Grow old on Saturn," he said. "Be my antennae. There's nothing for you here."

"What will you do?"

Reiss smiled thinly. "Blanca will need watching. He will be reluctant to forgive us for allowing Avon to kill his lover. I've taken steps to placate him, but I'll still have to be careful. Of course, if I'm right about the mood of our people, the Council may have to call on me. Blanca will be obliged to go along with the general consensus. When I'm called, I'll call for you.

"Meanwhile, I want you to trace Avon's movements. I want to know the name of everybody with whom he came into contact. Will you do that?"

Makarov nodded. "What was there about the man? Why were you so obsessed with the hunt for him?"

"We shared the same mother."

Makarov looked startled, frowned and pursed his lips. "You mean that the full resources of the Federation were activated so that you could pursue a personal vendetta?"

Reiss smiled at him. "More or less."

"The hurt must run very deep."

Reiss's smile faded.

Makarov shook his head wearily. "I find it difficult enough to cope with you as a friend. I should despair if you ever became my enemy," he said with feeling.

Reiss stood. "I'll arrange for your transportation to Saturn. Remember what I have asked of you."

"I will."

Reiss watched as the older man wheeled himself away. When he had gone, he turned on his heel and walked from the corridor in which their conversation had taken place and re-entered the Council chamber room.

Vasht was standing alone by one of the tall windows. It was wide open and a breeze from outside was ruffling her long red hair. It flattened her silk dress against her body, so emphasizing her superb figure.

Reiss stood beside her and looked out over the forbidding mountains. "Thank you," he said hoarsely.

"For nothing," she replied.

"On the contrary! You have removed Makarov from any sphere of influence. You have provided Blanca with an alternative to the Martian. Between us we have altered Council policy to your advantage and to my satisfaction."

"You really think that Gros is an adequate replacement for Pruth?"

"I assure you, his tastes are exotic. The White Cobra will take great pleasure in the black velvet mole."

Vasht laughed. But it was a hollow laugh that echoed through the chamber. She turned and placed her hand at a point just below Reiss's waist. She looked deep into his eyes for a reaction. There was none. She removed her hand.

Reiss walked away and sat on the edge of the magnificent desk. He stared up at the painting on the wall. He smiled to himself.

Vasht stood at his shoulder. "Rogue is dead. Surely it is all over?"

Reiss's long black lashes hooded his eyes. "Not until every trace of him has been removed from the Universe."

She placed an arm around him. Almost immediately, he stood, shrugging her off. She pouted at him. "What shall I do with his head?" she asked.

Reiss laughed.

"Where will you go now?" she pressed.

"To the Graveyard. That was where Avon gave us the slip after he had killed the Martian. The Guardian may have something to tell me."

The breeze had become a wind and gusts plucked at the heavy velvet curtains that hung by the high windows. It rattled a crystal chandelier attached to the ornate ceiling.

Vasht shivered and wrapped her arms around herself as she rocked to and fro on the edge of the desk, like a lonely child suffering from lack attention and lost in her own thoughts. In a way, that's exactly what she was.

Reiss, himself thoughtful, suddenly became aware of the gusting wind and closed the shutters. "Eerie, isn't it?" he said. "Here we are at the heart of the Federation body and there is silence. It is as if the heart has stopped beating."

Vasht dragged herself out of her reverie and assumed a businesslike tone. "The Full Council is scheduled to meet here tomorrow," she said, "to decide policy with regard to the fresh air of liberalism that seems to be pervading the atmosphere. The heart will beat strongly enough then."

Reiss sighed. "It's always the same. If you don't have a war or some other crisis, the people get bored and seek out a cause on which to expend their surplus energy. Suddenly, they become obsessed with a will o' the wisp called Freedom."

"Freedom from what?"

"The Federation. You and people like you. People like me, I suppose. They'll never really achieve it, of course. After all, the Federation, to coin a phrase, is the only game in town."

"In the Universe."

"Whatever!" Reiss said with a shrug.

"Go now," Vasht told him, "and try to stay alive."

Reiss looked once more at the painting on the wall. "What is it called?" he asked.

"The Garden of Earthly Delights."

Reiss laughed, his amusement quite genuine. "Whoever painted it certainly had a sense of humor."

Vasht frowned. She failed to see the joke.

3

During the course of three centuries, the Earth had been a battleground. Wars between races and nations had devastated its land masses, polluted its seas and atmosphere, decimated its population. Only a small part of the World remained habitable.

The humanoids who survived looked to other known planets for living space, for the key to their future.

Gradually, some sort of order was restored out of the awful chaos. An order based on the family system.

Nine families, their servants, their kinsmen, their bastards and their armies formed "The Federation."

Suspicious, superstitious, sometimes aggressive, the families only supported each other in the pursuit of conquest and in schemes that were mutually beneficial.

Reiss was a member of one of the families, Vasht of another.

As the Federation expanded into a Universal Empire, conquered races from Mars, Neptune, all the planets, were adopted, as it were.

Apart from coalitions in time of war or when some catastrophe threatened, the families rarely mixed. Only at the High Council table did their powerful representatives indulge in social intercourse.

Sometimes, two or more of the families joined forces against others that they considered too greedy or ambitious. Each family had a "business," and jealously guarded its interests.

The Gros family controlled drug manufacture, Vasht's built the spacecraft that flew them to the stars, Reiss's father had dealt in gold.

The only time it could be said that the families were truly at peace was when their various members were dead. Then they met in another place—the Graveyard.

It was from here that Rogue Avon had set out on his fateful journey to Earth and it was here that Reiss came to enquire after him.

The black Guardian, Mishka, received him cautiously. Conscious of Reiss's rank and reputation, Mishka feared him. Not without cause.

They walked through the same mortuary that Avon had visited and Mishka showed Reiss the empty Pod bay from where his visitor's enemy had been launched.

"You say he forced you at gunpoint to do what he asked?" Reiss enquired sceptically.

"Yes."

"He was surely a forceful man."

"Yes."

"You're a liar!"

Mishka froze beneath Reiss's icy glare. Then, he relaxed, prepared to accept any fate. "Yes."

Reiss smiled. "It doesn't matter. I can understand that you might have admired him. Seen in him something you wish you had in yourself."

"I envied him," Mishka said. "He was free."

Reiss thought for a moment. "Yes. I suppose, in a way, he was."

"He's dead." Mishka stated rather than questioned.

111

"Did he mention my name?" Reiss asked casually.

"No."

"Are you sure?"

"It was I who mentioned it."

Reiss's eyebrows rose. "Did you indeed? And what was his reaction?"

"It seemed as if a weight had been lifted from his shoulders. As if, at last, he understood something of great significance."

"In what connection did you mention my name?"

"The families were quarreling over the spoils of the wars for Uranus. This was common knowledge. You figured largely in the quarrel." He permitted himself a wry smile. "You overhear quite a lot when you are burying the relatives of the powerful."

Reiss smiled back at him. "Yes, I suppose you do."

"Of course," Mishka added hastily, "I have no one with whom to discuss matters. I am alone here."

"How do you bear it?"

"How do you?" the Guardian asked perceptively.

Reiss nodded his approval of the question, but was clearly not prepared to answer it. Instead, he said, "You should be advised that there is likely to be an increased demand for your services."

A shrill whining sound interrupted them.

"That's a signal that I am about to receive a message," Mishka said. "It's probably from one of the families."

Both men returned to the Guardian's living space where he extracted a disc from the console that housed his communication system. He studied it. "It's for you." he said.

He showed Reiss how to work the machine, then indicated that he would leave the room to ensure Reiss's privacy

The machine activated, a voice said, "This is Sabbath."

"Well?"

"I thought you should know that there is a woman, recently arrived on Saturn from the Raphael system. She has become associated with the surgeon, Pi Grant. What is significant is that I cannot trace her background. What is more significant is that she has enquired—discreetly, it must be admitted—about Rogue Avon."

Reiss's eyes narrowed. "Go on."

"She is accompanied by her young son."

"Name?"

"She is called Rowena. He is Kerguelen. The woman claims she was raped and never really knew the boy's father. However, we know that Avon ran from Uranus and entered the Raphael complex. It's an interesting coincidence."

"I don't believe in coincidence," Reiss said. "Of which family is Grant a member?"

"Of the Gros. Drugs. He is clearly putting his expertise to a humanitarian use. He's highly thought of, very rich, a touch liberal."

"Then he will become acquainted with Makarov?"

"Certainly."

"Doubtless, the woman will try to milk him of information concerning my half-brother. Tell me about the boy."

Sabbath chuckled. "Strangely, he looks a lot like you!"

4

If they were similar in no other way than in their family resemblance, Reiss shared with Rogue Avon an enduring quality—patience.

His vassal on Saturn—Sabbath—regularly reported to him on Rowen'a activities and informed him of the boy's progress. He also passed on information concerning the other Grants.

Most interestingly, he sent Reiss a secret medical report of Anna's visit to an independent psychoanalyst. It revealed that the girl was unstable. That there was a tiny element in her brain that unbalanced her judgment. The condition was being treated with drugs that were addictive. Reiss decided to use this information for his advantage.

When Del Grant left Saturn Major for the Iron School, Anna accompanied him on part of his journey in order to visit Titan, Jupiter's moon. It was there that she and Reiss became acquainted.

Later, when Makarov died, Reiss became deeply suspicious of the manner of his death and ordered Sabbath to conduct a private autopsy. Very faint traces of the toxic substance that Rowena had used to destroy her enemy were at last discovered.

Reiss was impressed. He had viewed holograms of the woman and admired her beauty. Now he found himself admiring her cunning and determination.

He took a keen interest in the boy and used any influence he had to ensure his successful progress. He smiled when notified of Kerr's unusual talents.

Only when the young man he had become convinced was Rogue Avon's son was ready to transfer to Earth, did Axel Reiss act.

He commanded that Sabbath destroy the entire Grant household at Saturn Major. Gave him carte blanche as to how this should be accomplished. Only Anna, he instructed, must be preserved.

Through her developing years, he had taken note of her growing relationship with Kerguelen.

On the eve of Rowena's destruction, almost on a whim, he decided he must see this woman for himself.

So it was that he, the instrument of her fall, was present at her death.

Subsidiaries attended Anna Grant before the blood orgy began. Through Sabbath, Reiss had ensured that she would become his creature for, unknown to any member of her family, the Coordinator had supplied her with an excess of the drugs to which she was rapidly becoming addicted. His task had not proved difficult. Socially acceptable as a means of relaxation and as aids to pleasure, hard drugs were easily obtainable. It was but a short step for Anna from simple pleasure to craven addiction.

Having seduced the young woman so that she might serve his purpose and shared with her Rowena's savage end, he now turned his attention to the young man— Kerr Avon.

In pitying the Anna who, in a drugged haze, giggled uncontrollably at the terrible sights he had set before her, it never occurred to Reiss that he might be deserving of a greater pity.

Through the years, he had nurtured his obsessional hatred of his half-brother.

Throughout the years, he had determinedly plotted to blot out every trace of his kin's existence.

115

Throughout the years, he appeared, to all intents and purposes, to maintain an admirable sanity.

In truth, the pain and tension of those years had driven him to madness.

5

Reiss took Anna Grant to Earth and entrusted her to Vasht's care.

He dispatched Sabbath to the Iron School to inform "Kerr Grant" of his family tragedy. The Coordinator had been instructed to place blame on dissidents with revolutionary ideals. He was to promise that retribution would be swift and sure. It would not be difficult to extract a "confession" from any number of Federation political prisoners.

In addition, Sabbath was to remain at the school as an instructor and, at the same time, observe Kerr's temperament and assess his abilities.

Reiss, each day bringing him greater control over Anna so that he could bend her to his will, promised her a reunion with her lover.

He viewed the prospect with relish. It would not be sufficient just to kill the youth. He must be manipulated and humiliated first.

Vasht was distressed by the clear alteration in Reiss's character. Well convinced of his cruelty and ruthlessness in the service of the Federation, she was alarmed by the revelation of the hitherto untapped depths of his malice.

She walked with him in the summer gardens of the castle of Lupus. Fountains sprayed ice cold water, fed to them by the mountains, on the surfaces of many ornamental pools. The scent of every imaginable flower filled the air.

"I feel like the consort of the Devil, strolling with him through the Garden of Eden," Vasht said, attempting to lighten Reiss's mood. He merely scowled.

Vasht touched his arm. "Leave it alone, Axel! Either that, or finish it now and forever!"

"When I'm ready and not before!"

"Of course," Vasht whispered to him, "Kerr Avon may finish you! I wonder if that is what you really want?"

Reiss replaced his scowl with a wry smile. "It's an interesting thought. It suggests that I can control my own fate. Temper the instrument of my destruction."

Vasht attempted to embrace him, but he pushed her away.

Much vexed, she said, "You forget. I know what Rogue did to you."

"I haven't forgotten."

"Does that mean that, in order to erase the memory, I will have to die too?"

"That's another interesting thought. But you're too bad to die." Reiss laughed humorlessly.

They walked on. Eventually, they seated themselves on stone benches and stared into the waters of a stream that ran past them. The stream was well stocked with fish, ready for the High Council supper table.

"You were right," Vasht said.

"I frequently am."

"The outer regions are in chaos," she continued, disdainful of his interruption. "There are guerrilla movements everywhere. Blanca has instituted severe measures, but there are elements, even here on Earth, that have found the courage to oppose them. The courts are

117

overcrowded." She smiled. "Even the Killer men cannot eliminate everybody."

Reiss made no comment.

"Gros has suggested we launch an expedition into the Beyond." Vasht continued. "It might serve as a distraction."

Reiss shook his head fatalistically. "It would certainly ease your problems if you could provoke a war with an alien civilization. If there is such a thing. Since the collapse of the superstition called religion, there is no fear of the 'unknown' to manipulate in order to control the mob."

Vasht was silent for a moment. Then, "Blanca wants you to take charge of the spy network. He wants you to root out all traitors."

"They would consider themselves patriots," Reiss said.

"He wants you to persecute dissidents and terrorists."

"They would call themselves freedom fighters."

Vasht flushed with anger. "What has freedom got to do with it? The Federation is all there is. There is no alternative. If there isn't a degree of freedom in the Federation system, it certainly won't be found anywhere else."

"Then your traitors and terrorists will try to change the system."

"We control it."

"Then they will fight until your control is lost and is found again by someone who commands their respect and support."

"You sound like a dissident yourself!"

Reiss scowled. "Know your enemy! I have had the luxury of knowing mine. Fight treason with deception, terror with counter terror. I have to tell you—you still might not win."

Vasht smiled ruefully. "Then, what's the point?"

Reiss looked at her searchingly. "The point is—there is no point?"

6

Despite reservations, Reiss did as he was bid and formed a group of dedicated followers who infiltrated all strata of Federation society on every planet, satellite and moon of the Empire.

Discontent was widespread and his success was minimal.

Those who were too influential to be simply murdered, or otherwise disposed of, had to be brought to trial. It proved necessary to manufacture charges, so that a kind of justice could be seen to be done. Any uprising that threatened to overthrow the regime, or disturb the status quo, had to be prevented at all and any costs.

Blanca achieved a greater reputation for extreme cruelty than any who had gone before him. His use of the most horrifying methods in suppressing the revolutionary zeal of those opponents of the system that Reiss brought to his attention caused him to become more widely known by his sobriquet—the White Cobra. He became a major target for assassins.

Mars and two of Neptune's moons flared in rebellion and a great battle was fought through the Clouds of Magellan. There was a slaughter on the satellite called Nereid.

When the battle was over, it was judged that the Federation had triumphed and it exacted awful retribution.

Nonetheless, some resistance survived and went underground.

On Earth itself, there was a sudden surge of antipathy to Blanca's methods, and those of the Counsellors who supported him. The threat of a new internecine conflict hung in the air.

The Federation backed away. It assumed an ersatz liberal conscience, pretended compassion, hid its terrible aspects.

Reiss, rejoining the ranks of the Killer men, conducted a secret, deadly campaign against its supposed enemies within. But, although his dedication to his task could not be faulted, he disliked the distraction from what he considered his main purpose.

However, Sabbath continued to keep him informed of Kerr's activities and of his steady progress through the ranks at the Iron School. The Coordinator arranged for Anna Grant to be housed in her natural brother's house and enabled her to resume her role of mistress.

Del Grant, conscripted into the Iron Guard and obliged to take part in the action fought in the Clouds, was wounded and listed as missing. In fact, he was captured by a guerrilla force on Nereid and converted to its cause.

Once more, Vasht met with Reiss in the gardens of Lupus. Now it was mid-winter and a thick carpet of snow covered the ground. The stream was frozen, as were the ornamental pools. Water from the fountain spouts had frozen in mid-flow, creating exotic ice sculptures. There was no scent from any flower and no birds sang.

Swathed in furs that only just succeeded in keeping out the fierce cold, they walked beneath trees stripped of their spring and summer glory.

"Blanca has become an embarrassment," Vasht said. "His excesses are bad for business."

Reiss said, "Tell me something I don't know."

"He must be removed from office," Vasht continued. "His resignation must be final."

"What makes you think he will resign?"

"You know what I mean!"

They stood together on the bank of the ice-covered stream. Vasht spoke quickly. "It would be preferred if none of the corporations appear to be involved. Some members of the Council will have to be appeased. I will undertake that task."

"I'm sure you'll handle it very well," Reiss said sarcastically.

Vasht ignored the remark. Although she spoke softly, almost as if she were discussing the weather, her concentration on the matter in hand was total.

"The execution must be carried out by someone who will have no difficulty gaining an audience. The assassin must be unarmed."

"Why don't you get to the point?" Reiss interrupted.

"You once told me that there is no point."

Reiss sighed irritably. "I'm too old, too tired and too intelligent for this prevarication."

"Very well," Vasht said. "Will you do it?"

"Do I have a choice?"

Vasht chose to ignore the question. "You are the one who is best placed. Blanca esteems you because of your recent successes. As far as he is able, he trusts you more than anyone. Except, perhaps, for Pel Gros. But that is a different kind of trust."

Reiss nodded thoughtfully. "How will Gros react?" He asked.

"You must kill him!"

"Two for the price of one?"

"You can name any price."

Reiss looked at her intently. "I think you're playing a game with me."

Vasht smiled beguilingly. "Why on Earth would I do that?"

"There is more than Earth at stake here."

"True."

Snow fell and Reiss looked up at the gray, threatening sky. "I'll do as you ask," he said at length, "But, let me make one thing quite clear. If I am taken after I have killed the White Cobra and his lover, and if I am, shall we say, accidentally killed by my captors or shot while trying to escape, I will have left instructions with people I trust to eliminate you!"

Vasht laughed. "That won't be necessary. I have a better scheme in mind."

"I'm listening."

"Killing Blanca and Gros will be a crime that cannot go unpunished. Federation justice must be done. You will be very popular with the masses, however."

Reiss scowled. "That I can do without!"

The snow was falling thick and fast, but neither of them seemed to notice.

"You are a faithful servant of the Federation," Vasht said, "I will decide the form your trial will take. I will suggest trial by combat."

Reiss looked at her, startled.

"It's an ancient ritual," she went on, "but it's quite acceptable."

"I thought our legal system was more civilized?"

Vasht shrugged. "The human race is too complex, too self-interested, too variable to understand the true meaning of the word. Barbarity lurks beneath its veneer."

Reiss smiled thinly.

122

"Your motive for the killings, though suspect, will
seem irrelevant," Vasht continued. "All you will have
to do to dismiss rumor and allay criticism is to fight and
win. You must accept a kind of exile. I guarantee it
will be comfortable, even luxurious."

"I have some unfinished business," Reiss said.

"Hear me out!" Vasht spoke sharply. "I will choose
your opponent for the combat." She paused, her eyes
gleaming as if in anticipation of intense sexual pleasure.
"I will choose Rogue Avon's son!"

Reiss threw his head back and laughed.

"Don't laugh too soon," Vasht interrupted him,
almost in a whisper. "He may kill you!"

Reiss took hold of her and pulled her to him in a
clumsy embrace. "Do you think I really care?"

7

It was arranged that Reiss would dine alone with
Blanca and Pel Gros. The latter still considered his
former ally a friend and the White Cobra admired him
as only a man of equal brutality could admire a con-
temporary.

Reiss was assigned a room in the castle of Lupus.
Preparatory to dressing in a simple, black velvet
coverall, he stripped naked and surveyed his body in a
long oval mirror.

His dark hair, cut in a fringe, framed a lined, pale
face. His eyes, deep in their sockets, were jet black,
unfathomable pools. The scars of many conflicts puck-
ered on his chest and back. One leg was slightly shorter
than the other, as a result of a wound sustained during

an attack upon him with a phosphorous grenade. His mid-section had been cut away. Flesh and bone had been replaced with a supple metal sheath. Artificial veins, inserted by skilled surgeons, allowed his life blood to flow between the upper and lower halves of his body. There were no other functioning organs. He was half a man.

He moved closer to the mirror so that his breath clouded his reflection. In his mind's eye, he recalled the day that his half-brother had torn him apart with a twin-bladed knife with serrated edge.

In the absence of a father, Reiss had assumed the role, but there had come a falling out between him and Rogue Avon that had been sudden and savage.

Avon had fled to Uranus with Reiss's blood on his hands.

A terrible cry constricting his throat, Reiss smashed the oval mirror. Blood from his fist mixed with powdered glass.

When he had brought himself under control, he bathed his wounded hand, dressed and walked out of the room. With measured tread, he made his way along a wide, brightly lit corridor that was walled with marble. At the end of it, he pushed open heavy panelled doors and entered the chamber of the High Council.

Blanca and Gros, seated at a table laden with every kind of food—meat, vegetables, rare fruits—rose to greet him.

"I'm sorry," Gros said in a hushed tone, "but I must search you for weapons. Just a formality."

Reiss smiled and raised his arms above his head while Gros, rather too perfunctorily, Reiss thought, patted his body with a certain effeminate grace.

Blanca nodded and smiled when he indicated that Reiss was unarmed and invited him to be seated.

"You have served us well," the albino said, picking at his food as if he considered eating a tiresome formality.

Reiss said nothing as Gros passed him a glass of Saturn wine.

Blanca cleared his throat. "Vasht tells me that you feel you have had enough. That you—how shall I put it?—that you wish to retire from our service. Is that so?"

Reiss nodded.

"Very few are permitted to retire peacefully from the ranks of the nine families," Blanca said ominously.

The sycophantic Gros sniggered.

"I was hoping you might allow an exception,"

Blanca frowned. "How old are you?"

"I really don't know. Perhaps fifty Earth years."

"A good age."

"Average as far as life expectancy in the Federation is concerned."

On cue, Gros laughed again.

"You understand, I'm sure," Blanca went on, "that, if we were to lose your services, they are likely to be sought by others?"

"I have no ambitions."

"That's not the point!" the albino snapped. "It is other ambitions that concern us."

"What do you propose?" Reiss was biting into a peach.

Blanca shrugged and glanced out of a high window at a full moon encased in a black night.

Gros leaned across the table and spoke earnestly. "Axel! There is great danger here. We have uncovered a plot."

"There are so many plots, I'm surprised you can tell one from the other," Reiss said acidly.

"Vasht is involved," Gros continued, then paused for a reaction.

Reiss smiled. "Isn't she always?"

"We wondered if she had approached you?" Blanca asked, his pink eyes narrowing to points.

Reiss looked from one to the other. "Of course," he said.

There was a sharp intake of breath from Gros.

Blanca was silent and very still, a glass of wine held halfway to his lips.

"As a matter of fact," Reiss said coolly, "she arranged our meeting here tonight so that I may kill you both."

Pel Gros, his face very pale, stood abruptly. Blanca grabbed his arm and, his concentration never leaving Reiss for a second, forced his companion to sit again. "And?" he said to Reiss.

Reiss stood, glass in hand, and glanced at the painting hanging on the wall at the far end of the room. "I considered it," he said.

"You're very frank." Blanca's eyes followed him like twin lasers homing in on a target.

"I see no point in deception," Reiss said, walking over to the painting, seeming to study it.

Blanca rose from the table and joined him.

Gros, tense and fearful, held his own wine glass in a grip of iron.

Reiss turned and smiled disarmingly. "It was a question of weighing the pros and cons," he said.

Blanca smiled conspiratorially. "I take it you have reached a sensible decision?" he asked coyly.

Reiss, his smile seemingly fixed in place, smashed his crystal glass on the edge of the Council's antique desk and slashed him across the face with jagged glass.

Blanca staggered back in surprise and pain.

Gros shrieked and leapt to his feet. Foolishly, he launched himself across the room at Reiss who, with the stiffened edge of his hand, cut him down with a savage blow.

Blanca, blood pumping from his eyes, was trying to reach an alarm button set into the wall.

Calmly, Reiss stripped himself of his wide leather belt studded with silver. He caught Blanca round the neck with it and forced him to his knees. The albino's eyes bulged. Now he choked on blood.

Gros, recovered, sprang across the desk and pushed the button. He turned and, transfixed with fear, watched as Blanca's body sagged beneath Reiss's powerful arms. With a twist of the belt, Reiss snapped the albino's neck. He turned his attention to Gros.

"No, No!" Gros whimpered as he backed away. He was frothing at the mouth.

Reiss struck him a terrible blow just above his heart and he fell. Reiss kicked his head. Then, grabbing him by his hair, he dragged him across the room to a high window.

Gros screamed as Reiss lifted him up and hurled him through the plate glass. He was still screaming as he fell to the gardens below.

The door to the chamber burst open and half a dozen Iron Guards piled into the room, their weapons levelled at Reiss.

Breathing heavily, stained with blood, he snatched a bottle of wine from the table and drained it.

Vasht entered. She viewed the scene with evident satisfaction. She walked over to Blanca's lifeless body and touched it with a dainty foot.

An icy wind gushed through the broken window. Tiny pieces of glass tinkled to the floor.

Vasht crossed the room to Reiss's side. He was sitting now. Outwardly calmed, his eyes bore into her. She leaned over and kissed him full on the lips.

PART FOUR

Desolation

1

Kerr Avon, known for the time being as Grant, learned well at the Iron School. The task his mother had set him weighed heavily but, for the moment, he devoted his time and energy to achieving that which would better equip him to carry it out.

He made no friends among the elite student body. Only Amiyak could be said to have a close relationship with him.

When Makarov died, there seemed to be no suspicion concerning the manner of his death and Avon, to whom subterfuge and cunning had become second nature, commiserated as a "Brother" should.

When they came to Earth together, they formed a bond of interdependence that would not be broken until Amiyak's death.

Because of its importance as a kind of insurance for the future of the Federation, the school and its

nhabitants were isolated and disciplined to the extent
that communication with the outside Universe was
severely restricted. Anna Grant was but a memory.

The day came when Sabbath came to call.

Quietly, very gently, for he too had a talent for
deception, he explained that Rowena and Pi Grant had
been murdered by dissidents. That the flame of revolu-
tion had been lit in the Empire and that they had been
among the first casualties. The perpetrators had been
caught, he said, tortured and executed. The quarters
of their mutilated bodies had been on public show and
Sabbath produced video films to prove it.

Avon's first question concerned Anna.

"She is safe," Sabbath answered him, smiling pater-
nally. "It was a happy accident that she was away from
her home at the time."

"Where is she?"

"Being cared for by powerful friends. In time, it may
be possible for her to come here. Difficult, given the
security that surrounds this place."

Avon seemed content with the answer. He went to
see Del Grant who was preparing to leave for the
Federation campaigns that would eventually lead to the
running battle through the Cloud of Magellan.

Never close, the two young men eyed each other
warily. Del asserted that he was satisfied that justice
had been done in the matter of the murder of his adoptive father and expressed little concern for Anna. "I
know she will be well looked after by Vasht," he said.

"Who?"

"Vasht is a member of the High Council. I am of her
family. We are related through my father who died on
Miranda."

There was an arrogance about Del that Avon found
distasteful. It would come as no surprise to him to learn

of his defection. He considered the man an opportunist. He would seek promotion and authority from anyone prepared to offer it. He was easy prey for sycophants, be they Federation or other. By failing to utilize his talents and for abandoning him on Nereid, the Empire would lose an eager Pandarus.

What neither of them knew was that Anna was being schooled by Vasht at the instigation of Axel Reiss. The innocent, unaffected girl would become a woman of devious and vengeful substance.

Sabbath took a personal interest in Avon. He taught forcefully and his pupil absorbed every hard lesson.

The Coordinator acquired a grudging respect for the growing man. In a report to Reiss, he described Avon as follows; "He is not tall. He is dark and melancholy. Although unable to compete physically with all his contemporaries, when 'outgunned' as it were, he backs off. Then, choosing his own time and battleground, when his adversary has been weakened, he strikes and invariably wins. When he loses, he revises his tactics, resolved never to lose again. He is a dangerous opponent. As amoral as a razor blade. He reminds me of you. He fights dirty!"

With the eruption of the revolutionary wars, that's exactly what Avon wanted to do—fight.

For all its conquests, the Federation had not subdued man's implacable enemy—time. This hung heavily on Avon, but his request for combat was denied.

As a sop to his injured pride and ambition, Anna was delivered to him at the Iron School. A grown woman, she was sleek and sophisticated and aloof. Only in their private moments together did her animal instincts, her voluptuous sexual appetite, manifest themselves.

Sabbath was amused, but approved of her ability to seduce Avon, to distract and manipulate him.

Not that he was easily distracted from a new infatuation—computers.

One sultry night, the two men were discussing the complex subject when Sabbath, under instructions from Reiss, chose to broach another. "Why do you not revert to your real identity?" The Coordinator asked casually.

Avon was immediately alert.

Sabbath smiled like a contented cat. "The Federation does not survive by ignoring its enemies."

There was a silence. Only the hushed whirring of delicate machinery distracted from it.

Avon's face was expressionless, his eyes hooded menacingly.

"We know that Rogue Avon ran from the wars for Uranus and found sanctuary on Phax. That's not all he found, of course. He found your mother, Rowena." Sabbath's smile seemed fixed in place, like the rictus of a cadaver. "You may not know," he continued, "that he was killed here, on Earth. For all his qualities, he was not for us. And those who are not for us, are against us and must be eliminated. Your schooling will ensure that you understand that."

"Who killed him?"

"Surely, you already know!"

Avon smiled.

"The Federation does not visit the sins of the fathers on their sons," Sabbath said. "The Empire values you and the service you can give it. In return, you will be well treated."

"Until my usefulness is at an end."

Sabbath pulled a face. "That applies to all of us."

"So, I am to be allowed to assume my own name without fear of retribution?"

"Yes."

"Why?"

"Let's say that the families prefer it that way. Your father was misguided. If you want to change the system, it is better to make the attempt from within."

"What about honor and conscience?" Avon asked.

"I doubt that you are familiar with either of them," Sabbath said, not unkindly.

Avon laughed.

"The Federation offers to create order out of chaos. I'm sure you approve of that. It also offers you in particular a way of life of your own choosing. Within reason, that is. After all, if I am not mistaken, you are for yourself. What do you care about the rabble?"

"You seem to have summed me up rather well."

"I've gotten to know you."

"I doubt that."

Sabbath made another face. "You are to be integrated into one of the families. That is a great privilege. I envy you."

"But?"

Sabbath grinned. "But! First, you have to prove something to us. The Iron Guard is preparing for an assault on Nereid, Neptune's satellite. There's a particularly nasty group of revolutionaries there. We would like you to join the expedition."

Avon thought for a moment, but his black eyes never strayed from their scrutiny of the Coordinator. "Very well," he said finally.

"You've made a wise choice," Sabbath said.

"I was unaware that I had one!"

"We leave tomorrow. Make the most of the night. It will be necessary to return Anna Grant to Lupus."

Avon nodded assent, excused himself and returned to his quarters. Anna was waiting for him. He told her of his conversation with the Coordinator. From this time on, she always referred to him as "Avon." The meaning

132

of his first name, she claimed, depressed her.

That night, they lay together as if the day that was surely to follow would never come. As if they were suspended in time and space. Frequently, Anna moaned that she loved him. Avon, who did not know the meaning of the word, could not bring himself to say it.

When the day did come, he left her when she was still asleep. Any reluctance was tempered with an instinct for self-preservation.

He took leave of Amiyak. His "Brother" wished him luck.

Avon said, "I'll make my own luck."

Amiyak frowned and placed an arm on his shoulder. "Then, may your God go with you."

"God has nothing to do with it!"

2

The terrible noise shattered her sleep and fragmented her dreams. Anna threw back the covers, sprang from her bed and, only then realizing that Avon had gone, rushed to a window.

Naked in the cold dawn, she watched as a score of heliplanes hovered over the school and its environs like a horde of locusts. One by one, they turned away and, their many-colored navigation lights flashing a farewell, flew off into the distance in search of the mother Starship that would carry them to Nereid.

The silence once they were gone was oppressive.

Unannounced, Sabbath came into the room. Anna turned to face him. Untroubled by modesty, she easily

133

withstood his hungry gaze. "What do you want?" she asked, then smiled when she considered that the question might be superfluous.

Sabbath said, "Avon has gone."

"I have eyes. I can see that!" she snapped, aware that her influence with Vasht and Axel Reiss placed the Coordinator as an inferior.

"You are to return to Lupus," he said.

Anna sighed, crossed to her bed and lay on it. She did not bother to cover her nakedness. She stretched voluptuously.

"I have been ordered to accompany Avon to Nereid," Sabbath went on, trying to control his desire and to ignore her abandonment.

"Why do you feel you have to tell me this?"

"Reiss wants to know if you have anything to report?"

She propped herself up on one elbow and stroked her breast with her free hand. "I'll tell him anything he needs to know myself."

Sabbath took a step forward. Anna's eyes hardened like gunmetal. "Touch me and you're dead!" she said viciously. "By Avon's hand or by that of Axel Reiss."

The Coordinator hesitated. "What if Avon should not return from Nereid?"

"Then you had better not return yourself."

"What if he discovers what really happened to his mother?"

Anna smiled. A smile on the face of a tigress. "He and I have shared this bed. I have the heart of the man. He would pluck out yours!"

Sabbath tried to ingratiate himself. "I can see that I have underestimated you," he said.

Anna did not reply. She turned away from him as if bored with their conversation.

The Coordinator, overcoming the anger he felt at the dismissal she implied, left her.

Having made sure that he had gone, Anna turned her face to the wall. There were acid tears in her eyes.

Sabbath would have been unimpressed. As it was, he concentrated on the matter in hand. He had to keep Avon alive and reckoned that might not be an easy task when fighting a war through the endless night of Nereid.

The satellite was unwelcoming. Its landscape was untamed. Its mountains huddled over great chasms. Its vegetation of thick and thorny scrub held the promise of death. The waters of its rivers and lakes was acid. Its atmosphere was barely breathable. It was an awful place. Because its mother planet, Neptune, blotted out the Sun, there was no day.

The Federation plan, such as it was, required two detachments of Iron Guards. One would press towards the center of the satellite from its North, the other, obliquely, from the South. The dissidents would be crushed between the two wings. This was easier planned than executed.

It soon became apparent that the scheme was unworkable. The terrain was impossible. The rebels appeared, struck hard, then disappeared like wraiths. One of their tactics was quite deadly as far as the intruders were concerned. A sniper would fire a projectile from a narrow tube, no thicker than a stem of bamboo. Provided the tube followed any evasive movement the target might make, the projectile, powered by gas and guided by a simple, narrow laser beam, would alter course accordingly. On impact, it would blow its target to pieces. Avon's troop lost two officers to this weapon within hours of their arrival.

"This is a waste of time and good men," Sabbath said

when he and Avon met in the satellite's Federation base. "Who wants a Godforsaken place like this anyway?"

Avon smiled. "Clearly, somebody does."

"The sooner we get out of here, the better."

"We'll see what tomorrow brings."

Sabbath spat on the ground. "There is no tomorrow here."

While the Coordinator and the rest, apart from a warning guard, slept, Avon wandered the compound. He sniffed the acrid air, shivered in the cold, but remained alert, all his senses honed to perfection by his many years of Federation tutelage in the art of war.

A Nereidian captive had been assigned to him as a servant. A slight man, in every sense of the word, he was called Paroch.

In the dead of what passed for a Nereidian night, he approached his new master. His voice was thin and reedy, his tone subservient, but there was a hint of steel in his suppliant eyes. "You are called Kerguelen?" he asked.

"Yes," Avon said, concealing his surprise that the slave knew his proper name. Avon was ever adept at controlling and hiding his feelings.

"I am in contact with your enemies," Paroch said.

Avon looked at him sharply. The man had just signed his death warrant.

"I would bring you to them," the servant muttered. "I have been instructed to do so. One of our leaders claims he knows you."

"So, you are one of them?"

"Yes."

"What is the leader's name?"

"Starets."

Avon shook his head.

"I have an image of him," Paroch said while producing a photograph and passing it over.

After studying it for a moment, Avon handed it back. "When?" he asked.

"When what?"

"When shall I see this man?"

"Tomorrow."

"Tomorrow never comes."

"Within another Earth day," Paroch said testily.

Avon nodded his assent. "Very well."

"You do not sleep?" Paroch enquired.

"I have a suspicion that those of us who indulge in the luxury of sleep here on Nereid may never wake."

Paroch smiled toothlessly. "You are very wise."

"I am careful."

"The Federation cannot conquer here," the slave said passionately.

"You're right. I think it may change its mind and decide to abort the mission."

Paroch giggled.

Avon dismissed him. When he had been obeyed, he lay back on his couch, his arms cradling his head.

Although it was a recognition of long ago, he had immediately remembered the face of the man in the photograph.

The assignation that Paroch had arranged would be with the Prospector.

3

They came to a deep cave. Hidden from the air, it was protected from detection devices by the non-reflective

137

granite of the mountain that contained it.

Stalactites dripped chill water on its spongy floor. Its atmosphere was fetid.

Nonetheless, it housed and provided sanctuary for enemies of the Federation. There were very few in this band, Avon noted.

Ill-clad, dirty and dishevelled, they exuded an air of hopeless defiance. The defiance of men with their backs to the wall and with nowhere else to go, prepared to fight to the last drop of blood because they had no alternative.

Starets, the Prospector, walked out of the murky cavern depths and stood before him. He still resembled an ancient prophet.

"So!" Starets said, his voice thin and quavering. "You are the child."

"Now I am a man."

Starets looked at the gun hanging from Avon's belt and smiled. "And you have put away childish things?"

Avon smiled too and the old man was convinced of his identity. It was a smile the Prospector, or anyone else, was unlikely to forget.

They sat together on wooden logs and one of Starets' followers brought them food and drink.

"Quite like old times," the ancient said. "Do you remember the sanctuary on Phax?"

"Yes."

"It is good that you remember. That is all there is. Memory."

Avon was silent.

"You're mother is dead." It was not a question.

"How do you know?"

The old man stroked his beard. "There was some fighting on Saturn. The Iron Guards from the military college suppressed the dissidents. News travels fast in revolutionary circles."

"Her killers were executed," Avon said.

Starets raised an eyebrow. "Really?"

Avon's eyes narrowed. "That is what I was told."

"You were misinformed."

There was a dread silence between them.

"Enlighten me," Avon said finally.

"Subsidiaries were responsible for her death," the Prospector said quietly. "Subsidiaries controlled by Earthmen."

Avon appeared to be calm. "Their names?" he asked politely.

"Are you sure you want to know?"

"I'm sure."

"Axel Reiss and his creature, the Saturn Coordinator."

"Sabbath!"

"Yes."

Avon stood and slowly paced the floor of the cave.

"Why don't you fight with us?" Starets asked. "Others have been persuaded."

Avon stopped pacing, looked at him and smiled coldly. "You and your kind don't stand a chance."

The Prospector was unmoved. "You contradict yourself. Here on Nereid, we will win."

"You're very welcome to this satellite. But try and move away from it and the Federation will annihilate you."

Starets frowned. "I could have you killed."

"Will you?"

The old man shook his head wearily. "I think you will do greater service to our cause by returning to your Federation masters. You will be a cancerous tumor in its political brain. One of many, I hope."

"I've heard something like that before."

Starets sighed. "Destruction such as you have seen and will continue to see is the prerogative of the human race. It is almost a vocation. In the end, the race will destroy itself. You are a symptom of its disease."

"I'm flattered."

Both men laughed.

"The Federation will continue to fight," the old man said, "but, as you say, they will eventually concede Nereid to us. You only have to look around you to know it will be a hollow victory. In a hundred years from now, what will it matter?"

Avon smiled.

The Prospector's eyes bore into him. "Of course, we all have to die."

"Yes. But how, when and by whose hand is of some importance."

"Is it?" the old man said drily.

Avon changed tack. "How could you be sure that I would believe what you have told me of the circumstances of my mother's death?"

Starets seemed irritated by the question. Like a man discomfited by an inquisitive child. "Believe or not believe, it's up to you." His mouth curled in a sinister smile. "The name Axel Reiss in connection with the affair should serve to convince you."

Avon nodded. "Reiss flits in and out of my life like a malevolent spirit. He has orphaned me. He must have had a good reason. Sooner or later, I'll kill him. Or die in the attempt."

"Why?"

"I gave my word."

The Prospector seemed approving, but he said, "Most men's 'words' are worthless."

"I am not most men."

The ancient rose to his feet. "You have illustrated

140

that by coming here. Do you give credence to prophecy, astrology?"

"No."

"Perhaps it's just as well. I don't see a particularly happy future for you."

"Then, why tell me and spoil my hopes?" Avon asked.

"What does it matter?"

"What do you see for yourself?"

The old man did not answer. Instead, he plucked two gold coins from the sleeve of his coat. "I think you should have these. Before the inflation of the last decade, they were worth a considerable amount in Federation credits. Although I would estimate that you are lacking in sentiment, take them anyway. They were given to me by a woman called Mara."

Avon accepted the coins.

"Go now!" The old man coughed as he spoke. "Paroch will guide you."

"Thank you," Avon said.

"For what?"

Avon shrugged. "For sparing my life perhaps?"

"I don't think I've spared you anything!"

4

Fulfilling expectations, the Federation ordered a withdrawal from Nereid, which now became a stronghold of sorts for dissidents, rebels, revolutionaries, political refugees and, inevitably, murderers and other fugitives from justice.

Avon and Sabbath, neither having fired a shot in

anger, returned to Earth and the Iron School.

The Coordinator reported to Reiss that Avon had conducted himself well throughout the abortive campaign, but that the true test of his mettle was still to come.

Anna Grant was gone. She was unwilling to return to the rigid atmosphere of the elite training ground, Sabbath said. She preferred the pleasures offered by the many mansions of Lupus.

Avon brooded.

On his second day on Earth after the retreat from Nereid, he received a visitor.

The stranger was a representative of one of the nine families. A family that controlled a business essential to Federation well being—money.

Maco, a slight, thin, sickly man, wore deep-lensed spectacles to compensate for fast-failing eyesight. As a member of the Seventh family, he was one of those who supervised the banking system and protected the Federation reserves of precious stones and metals.

He seemed subservient, but there was an edge to his voice and a kind of authority in his magnified eyes.

"I has been brought to my attention," he said, "that you have, shall we say, a flair for, and an understanding of, the science of mathematics. That you comprehend the philosophy of the subject and do not consider it a matter of mere figures."

"I could almost describe it as an art," Avon interrupted.

Maco smiled approvingly. "Quite."

Avon waited for him to continue and his guest shifted uncomfortably in his chair as he opened a file and tried to read it with the limited assistance of his lenses. "You are rather young," he said. "Twenty-six Earth years."

"More or less."

"What does that mean?" Maco said sharply. "Mathematics requires you to be precise."

"Very well, I'm twenty-six Earth years."

"You look older."

"I've led an interesting life."

"Please, don't be flippant."

"Then, why don't you say what you have come to say?"

"I shall."

Avon poured his visitor a glass of Saturn wine. He drank water himself. This did not go unnoticed.

"You are probably aware," Maco said, somewhat pompously, "that the Federation has experience a certain amount of, shall we say, turmoil over the last decade. Fortunately, there are those among the families who are able and prepared to pluck order from chaos and who are equally prepared to utilize their talents for the benefit of all."

"But mainly for themselves!"

Maco smiled slightly. "Quite! I see that we have something in common."

Avon refurbished his drink.

Maco assumed a serious expression. "You have no family?"

"Not any more."

"Good. I mean, I am sorry, but good from our point of view."

"Which is?"

"We would like, shall we say, to adopt you."

"The Federation seems prepared to adopt everyone."

"The Federation creates many orphans."

"And wishes to be the mother of its invention."

"Quite!"

"Who sent you?"

"I thought I mentioned I was from the Seventh

family?"

"You didn't, but I believe you. I ask again, who sent you?"

Maco smiled secretively. "Vasht."

"How am I supposed to react?" Avon asked casually.

"You can accept the offer."

"What exactly does it entail?"

Maco folded his hands in his lap and assumed the aura of a stern grandparent. "I will introduce you to the mysteries of high finance. If you prove an apt student, I will unravel them for you. Once you are, shall we say, qualified, you will serve the Federation and, of course, be of especial service to the Seventh family."

"Are there any, shall we say, additional services expected of me?"

Maco spread his hands in a gesture that suggested what he was about to say was of little importance. "The family business needs protection. Your other talents will provide that."

"You mean I'm considered suitable for the ranks of the Seventh family's Killer men?"

"How quickly you grasp the situation."

"I take it you are having problems with the other families?"

Again, Maco shifted uncomfortably. "In a word—yes!"

"There have been rumors."

Maco became quite animated. "Since the wars for Uranus, there have been many shifts in power and influence. For the moment, and I trust it is only a moment, Blanca and Pel Gros control, as it were, the reins of terror."

At the mention of Pel Gros, Avon's eyes narrowed. Again, this did not go unnoticed.

Maco continued, "Our family is becoming a little

tired of playing second fiddle to the White Cobra and his lover. We seek our place—how shall I put it?—our place in the sun."

"A worthy ambition."

"I'm glad you think so. However, ambition must be made of sterner stuff than we are at present. So, we turn to you and others like you. Will you favor us by joining the family?"

"If I do, will this be a disfavor to Pel Gros?"

"Indubitably."

"In that case, you have my word."

"Thank you. Vasht will be pleased."

"I looked forward to meeting her."

Maco eyed the young man approvingly, then smiled his secret smile. His pebble glasses reflected dully. "I have a suspicion that that meeting will be, shall we say, interesting."

"When do we leave?"

"Tomorrow," Maco replied promptly.

"That's acceptable. I have something to attend to before we go. It shouldn't take long." Avon extracted a twin-bladed knife with serrated edge from its sheath.

Maco blinked furiously. "Nothing too dangerous, I hope?" His voice was hoarse.

Avon smiled.

5

If hands can perform the art of healing, it follows that they can be trained as instruments in the equal art of killing.

The Iron School's gymnasium provided the

environment for the learning of such skills.

Sabbath was a master of unarmed combat. His hands, tenderly cared for, were weapons as lethal as any gun or knife.

Stripped to the waist, his oiled body gleaming, his muscles firm with tension, he was instructing Amiyak in the finer points of self-defense. He was attacking.

Amiyak reeled under a swift succession of terrible blows. He scrambled away as Sabbath executed any number of threatening, balletic movements. Should the Coordinator wish it, he could easily break the man. Amiyak was not his most gifted pupil.

"Enough!" Sabbath said and Amiyak permitted himself a sigh of relief.

The Coordinator placed his arm round the young man's shoulders. "You're improving," he said, "but your heart isn't in it. Remember, there is a marked difference between men. There are those who are skilled, even expert, who can be overcome by a lesser opponent. The difference being that, where one man may use these skills simply to survive, another is excited by challenge. He intends, wants, needs to kill. That's an edge you are lacking. But, you have other abilities. If you hadn't, you wouldn't be here."

"You mean, I don't have a psychological aptitude for murder?" Amiyak said.

The Coordinator looked at him severely. "What I'm saying is, once armed with the skill, if you hesitate to use it, you're dead."

"It seems a poor substitute for diplomacy."

Sabbath held up his hands. "These are my diplomats."

Amiyak smiled. "Yet you and others like you are the lesser men. Vassals of others less talented in the field in which you seem to be expert. Why is that?"

Sabbath frowned.

Amiyak placed a finger to his temple. "This is my diplomat. I use my brain. Fraud before force, Coordinator!"

Sabbath said nothing, but his eyes betrayed irritation and a hint of contempt.

Amiyak extended his hand in a gesture of friendship. Sabbath ignored it.

The younger man shook his head sadly and turned away.

In the corridor outside the training room, Avon was waiting. He and Amiyak faced each other.

Avon, his head to one side as if listening for something that only he would hear, smiled. Then, he brushed past his "Brother" and entered the gymnasium, closing the door behind him.

Sabbath, flat on his back, was pushing heavy weights above his chest, flexing his powerful muscles, bulging his neck with effort. His eyes acknowledged Avon's presence, but he continued his exercise.

Avon leaned casually against a padded vaulting horse and watched him. The Coordinator, anxious to impress, succumbing to vanity, performed with flamboyant skill and strength.

Avon took a step towards him.

On either side of Sabbath's prone body, stood two rests for the heavy iron weight he was pumping. Avon kicked them away. Sabbath, his eyes rolling with the pain of exertion, his surprise total, released the weighted bar so that it crashed onto his chest, pinning him to the floor. He screamed in agony. Both men heard the cracking of his ribs. The Coordinator was bathed in sweat, heaving with pain.

Avon removed his twin bladed knife with serrated edge from the sheath concealed behind his back. He spoke very quietly, but clearly and menacingly. "You will answer a number of questions," he said. "I will cut off your fingers one by one until I am satisfied. Do you understand?"

Sabbath, his face creased with the effort of withstanding the growing intensity of pain, gritted his teeth and attempted to speak. His mouth failing to form the words, he could only nod.

"You killed my mother, Rowena?"

The Coordinator's answer was a strangled cry, "No!"

Avon's eyes grew dark. His voice was a hoarse whisper. "Remember, Sabbath, there are some men excited by challenge. Men who intend, want, need to kill."

"Subsidiaries." Sabbath hissed.

"Under your command?"

"Yes."

"And Axel Reiss?"

"Yes."

Avon turned and walked out of the room into the corridor. Amiyak stood by the door. Avon held out his hand. "I'll take the gun now."

Amiyak, after a moment's hesitation, produced a heavy recoilless weapon and passed it to him. "I has six shots," he whispered.

"I'll only need one."

Avon returned to the gymnasium and Sabbath. The Coordinator was struggling desperately in an attempt to rid himself of the crushing weight of the iron bar.

Avon pointed the gun at his face, aiming at a point directly between the eyes. Sabbath froze, his expression slightly comic as he tried to include both the gun and his persecutor in the breadth of his vision.

"I remember you once told me," Avon said, "that you admired a man who could be patient. A man who would wait until his enemy was weakened and vulnerable. A man who would choose his own time, select his own killing ground. You have taught me well. But for you, Sabbath, here endeth the lesson!" He squeezed the trigger and the gun roared.

As the deadly echoes faded, another sound intruded and Avon whirled around, levelling the weapon at Amiyak who had entered the room behind him. His "Brother" recoiled in horror and turned his face away, sickened by the sight of Sabbath's mangled body.

Avon said, "You're going to tell me that he was unarmed, helpless. That I gave him no chance."

Amiyak's expression conveyed revulsion leavened with contempt. He was deathly pale, his eyes wide with grief and terror.

Avon said reflectively, "He was a hard man. If I'd given him only half a chance, he might have killed me instead. Remember that! Winning is what counts. The end justifies any means."

"I can't accept that," Amiyak said breathlessly.

"Then, you won't live long!"

Amiyak leaned against a wall as if afraid that his legs would no longer support him.

Avon tossed the gun on the floor. "Maco is taking me to Lupus," he said, "where I'll learn the finer arts." He looked down at the Coordinator's body. "In the end, though, it will always come to this."

Amiyak seemed on the verge of tears. "Then, there is no hope for us."

"There's always hope. But, when you live in exciting times, don't always expect your hopes to be fulfilled."

Amiyak moved closer to him. "You're a dead man!" he said.

"Oh, I think the Federation might be prepared to overlook this, shall we say, aberration. They might

149

even approve of it."

"I mean, you're alive but, inside yourself, you are cold and dead."

"That's a discomforting thought!"

Amiyak spat at him. "You're the face of the Federation that I can no longer bear to look at," he said viciously.

The door to the gymnasium, which was ajar, creaked on its hinges. Amiyak jumped like a startled deer. Avon remained motionless.

"I hope I'm not intruding?" Maco said, as he stepped into the room. His eyes, hidden behind his thick-lensed glasses, flicked from one man to the other and finally came to rest on Sabbath's corpse. "I take it we are free to go now?" he asked blandly.

Avon, after a last look at Amiyak, walked out on them.

Maco pursed his lips. Managing to control his obvious distaste, he knelt to take a closer look at the body. "Avon is nothing if not thorough," he said.

Amiyak snorted his disapproval.

"Ah! I see you don't share my admiration." Maco said lightly. "Well, never mind." He rose to his feet. "You must admit, he is a little more practical than you or I. On the other hand, the brute is more susceptible to guile than we other men. Be assured that Avon's weaknesses will be exposed and exploited."

Amiyak looked puzzled. "I thought he was to join the Seventh family?"

"True."

"And that you are his mentor!"

Maco removed his glasses and began to polish them. "Surely you have learned by now," he said, "we are none of us what we seem!"

There was a long silence while Maco finished his

polishing and replaced his glasses astride his nose. He smiled conspiratorially. "Unfortunately for you," he said, not unkindly, "you have, shall we say, a conscience. Admirable in any other age, at this time it is a forbidden luxury."

"What's that supposed to mean?"

Maco's voice took on a hard edge. "That's for you to find out." His eyes flicked to the doorway. Two Iron Guards had entered. Maco smiled thinly. "For some reason best known to himself, Axel Reiss harbors an incurable hatred for Avon's family and comrades. Poor Avon! Unfortunately, I was unable to prevent this." He waved a hand in the direction of the stiffening corpse. "But I can fulfill my other obligations."

The Iron Guards stood either side of Amiyak.

"You show no fear. That's good." Maco said. "You understand, I hope, that I am merely obeying orders? That there is no personal ill feeling?"

"I understand, but I doubt Avon will. He takes everything personally."

Maco laughed. "Quite! An astute observation."

Amiyak forced a smile. "I hope, for your sake, that no one underestimates him. Sabbath did!"

Maco eyed him thoughtfully. "I'll be careful." He nodded and the Iron Guards took hold of Amiyak, prepared to drag him away. In the event, he was docile and allowed himself to be taken quietly from the room.

Maco, without a backward glance at the dead Sabbath, shortly followed. Later, he and Avon boarded a heliplane that would take them to the Federation's capital.

"Would you consider Amiyak a friend?" Maco asked, his voice straining in competition with the noise from the aircraft's rotors.

"I have no friends."

151

"How unfortunate."

"For whom?"

Maco removed his spectacles and appeared to study them. Both men knew he could not see without them. "Why did you kill Sabbath? he asked politely.

"Don't you know?"

"How could I?"

"Didn't your master tell you?"

"Who?"

"Axel Reiss."

Maco tensed. "I serve Vasht. It was she who sent me."

Avon leaned across and took the glasses. "You should always wear these," he said. "Otherwise, you will never see clearly!"

"Amiyak warned me not to underestimate you," Maco said quietly.

"You wouldn't be the first. You won't be the last."

"I wonder if we might come to an arrangement?" Maco asked, retrieving his glasses from Avon's grasp.

Avon smiled. "I'm open to suggestions."

"You have correctly surmised that I am an agent of Axel Reiss. Although, it is true that Vasht gave me my instructions on his behalf. This suggests an intelligence that I hadn't given you credit for. In addition, you have indicated that you have a harsh commitment to violence. I think, under the circumstances, I would rather have you as a friend than an enemy. Could you bring yourself to trust me?" Maco looked directly at Avon, his glasses and serious expression combining to suggest he was giving an impression of an aged owl.

"Perhaps." Avon said.

"Then, in order to illustrate that I have a harsh commitment to you, I will tell you something you need to hear. You won't like it, but it is the truth."

Avon was silent.

"Anna Grant was present when your mother was murdered."

Avon did not move a muscle. It seemed as if he had stopped breathing.

Maco eyed him fearfully. "Reiss controls her. Vasht is her protectress."

Avon said nothing.

"What will you do?" Maco asked carefully. "Whatever you decide," he added hastily, "you can count on my assistance."

The heliplane's engine changed its rhythm and tone. It was beginning its descent into Lupus.

"Be very wary," Maco said intently. "They mean you harm."

Avon smiled wearily. His eyes alone conveyed his pain and disappointment.

The aircraft landed and, once they had disembarked, took off again. The wind created by its rotor blades almost jerked them off their feet.

They stood and looked into the distance at the castle that housed the High Council of the Federation.

"Impressive, isn't it?" Maco said.

Avon's dark eyes, like a serpent's, slid over him. "Is Reiss here?"

"No."

"Is Anna Grant?"

"I think so."

A troop of Death Squad guards trotted towards them from the castle grounds.

"Vasht will be here," Avon said.

"Certainly."

"Good."

The Death Squad troopers drew closer.

"Remember," Maco whispered, "getting into Lupus has proved relatively easy. Getting out might pose a

153

problem."

The troopers surrounded them.

"I think they want us to accompany them." Maco said.

Avon stood quite still, apparently studying their reception committee with interest.

An officer stepped forward. He deferred to Maco. "You are expected," he said. He turned to Avon. "Who is this man?"

Maco smiled benignly. "A friend."

There were several ominous clicks as the troopers primed their weapons.

Maco was nervous. His hands fluttered protest. "I assure you that Vasht expects him as well," he said eagerly.

The officer had not taken his eyes of Avon. "Why have you come here?" he asked.

"Well," Avon said, quite unabashed, "it seemed like a good idea at the time!"

6

The Death Squad troopers separated the two men. Maco was escorted to the castle. Avon remained with the officer and four others. Without warning, one of the troopers hit him in the groin with the butt of his laser rifle. Avon doubled up in agony, his vision blurred, nausea all but overwhelming him. The officer grabbed his hair, yanked him to his feet and slapped him hard across the face. Then the troopers lifted him, carried him several hundred meters to a small house and stood him between them as the officer unlocked a door. Then they propelled him forwards and he received a vicious kick in the back. He stumbled through the open door into the house, fell to the ground and lay still. The officer kicked him once more and he lost consciousness.

When he came to, he was in Anna Grant's arms. The pain in his head was almost unbearable, his senses nearly deadened. But he could smell her clean, seductive perfume, feel her soft body against his, hear her whispered endearments, taste her kisses.

With a supreme effort, he flung her from him. She lay next to him, her fingers clutching the ground, her eyes blazing.

Avon staggered to his feet. Anna crawled to him and grasped his leg. He kicked her aside.

The room seemed to move, he could hardly see. He stumbled to a nearby door and crashed it open. The room beyond was a bathroom. He took icy water from a standing jug and poured it over his head. His pain receded.

He glanced at his reflection in a mirror. His face was bruised, cut and swollen, blood caked his mouth. One eye was almost closed.

A slight sound made him turn. Anna stood close by, her face creased with anxiety, her eyes soft and appealing. She was either a consummate actress, or she cared for him. She held out a bottle of liquor. Avon snatched it from her and drank deeply.

Tentatively, she approached him, took his hand and led him to a large, luxuriously furnished room. She laid him down on a couch and sat alongside him. Her long fair hair practically touched his face. Her face hovered over him like a sad moon. She touched his brow. Avon closed his eyes and drifted into sleep.

When he woke up, he was alone. He stood and the

room was still. His eyesight was normal. He discovered that he was naked under a long silk robe. He crossed to the bathroom and once more surveyed himself in the mirror. His cuts and bruises had been carefully tended. The swellings had gone down.

When he stepped back into the room, Anna was lying on the couch. Leaning on one elbow, her face propped in her hand, she was watching him intently.

Avon leaned against the door jamb. "How long have I been here?" he asked, his voice thick.

"An Earth day."

"Who cleaned me up?"

"I did."

Avon snorted in disbelief.

"Some troopers helped me," Anna said quietly.

Avon rubbed his eyes as if to dispel an unwanted vision. Anna sat up. He took a step towards her, his hands clenched into fists, his face taut with anger. "How did my mother die?" he asked through clenched teeth.

Anna sprang to her feet and crossed to a desk set against a wall. She opened a drawer, took out several phials and syringes and placed them on the desk top. She stepped away, her back to the wall.

Avon walked over to her. He took one of the phials, opened it and sniffed its contents. He took a little of the fine white powder it contained and tasted it. He looked up sharply. "How long?" he asked.

Anna shrugged. "Long enough."

"Since Saturn?"

She nodded.

"Before I left for Earth?"

Again she nodded. Tears appeared at the corners of her eyes.

Avon crushed the phial in his hand. Anna stepped

forward and he took her in his arms. She spoke to him in a whispered rush of words. He could hardly hear her.

"When I was a child, unknown to anyone of our family, I became ill. It was a sickness of the mind. This was my treatment. It was Sabbath who supplied me, but he wouldn't help unless I did something in return. He was using me on behalf of Axel Reiss. I'm still being used. I'm supposed to be a distraction for you here. To soften you up so that they can kill you."

Avon was unconvinced. "They can do that any time they like," he murmured.

"I knew nothing of what was to happen at Saturn Major." Anna continued. "They killed Pi Grant because he would more than likely learn of my addiction and begin to ask difficult questions of Sabbath and Reiss. They killed Rowena because Reiss knew she had been with the traitor Rogue Avon and that you were his son by her. I begged them not to do it. I tried to stop them. You must believe me!" She smothered him with kisses. She wept uninhibitedly.

Avon led her to the couch and they lay down upon it, clutching each other like frightened children. "Take me away from here," Anna begged through her tears. "I love you. I would never have willingly hurt you. I'll never hurt you again. You must believe me!" She kissed him again. Her hands grasped the cord of his robe and she tore the garment off him. She crushed her body against his, forced him to love her.

When it was over, they lay naked together. The room was in darkness. Their faces were very close. Anna's eyes were wide and innocent. Avon could not doubt that she loved him. He kissed her mouth, her eyes, her breasts.

Avon stood, wrapped his silk robe around him and

157

retrieved the bottle of liquor from the desk. He shared its contents with her. "Sabbath is dead," he said finally.

Anna sighed.

"I can't work out why I have been brought here," he said, "perhaps you can guess?"

"I've already told you. They mean to kill you."

Avon frowned. "This is the heart of the Federation. My life is worth nothing here. Why haven't they killed me already?"

"I don't know."

Avon stood and began to pace the room. "Three men were responsible for my father's death. Rowena found out about them and sought vengeance. She became obsessed. Makarov was one of them. She poisoned him. Before I left Saturn, she made me swear to kill the others. I can't break the promise. I intend to keep it."

"And then?"

Avon smiled. "I have no plans."

"We could run," Anna said.

"Where? There is only Federation space."

"We could run to the Children."

Avon stopped pacing. Anna ran to him and placed her arms around him.

"Who or what are the Children?" he asked.

"Seven planets in no man's space between the Empire and the Beyond. In the Eastern sky. They are called the Children because they are satellites of Jupiter, the father. But they orbit far from the planet and well away from Federation space lanes." She moved away from him and turned on a dim light. Her naked body seemed ghostly in its glow.

"Why hasn't the Federation conquered the Children like everywhere else?"

"The satellites have nothing to offer. They are

sanctuaries for the very rich and are self-supporting, but they have no precious metals or stones. Nothing worth fighting for. Of course, the Federation attempted an invasion and landed troops on one of the Children. They were annihilated. It attacked again in greater force, but the inhabitants, rather than surrender, exploded a nuclear device that devastated the satellite and wiped out any number of the invaders. This was too high a price for the Federation to pay, so a truce was negotiated. The Children are independent and ignored. The destruction of the eighth satellite ensured the survival of the remaining seven."

"And there is where you want to run?"

Anna took his face in her hands and smiled up at him. "There is nowhere else."

"What will it take?"

"The Children have a High Council, too. We must appeal to it for sanctuary."

"We might be rejected."

She kissed him. "Not if we have money."

"Why would the Children need money?"

"Some things must be bought. They must also buy off any adventurers that might threaten them, Federation or otherwise. Money is the army that guards their independence."

"How much would we need?"

"A lot."

Avon smiled. "And where do you proposed we get it?"

"We can withdraw it from the banking system. A system controlled by the Seventh family."

"Of which I am now a member?"

"Yes." Anna laughed gaily. Avon grabbed hold of her and kissed her passionately. She broke away, snatched up her robe and wrapped herself in it. "We must eat," she said, "I have food and drink for us." She glanced at the drugs lying on the desk. "Will you help me?" she asked, her voice seeming to come from afar off.

"Yes."

"Will you love me, protect me?"

There was a long pause before Avon said, "Yes."

Her face radiant, she kissed him, then bustled about the room preparing a meal for them.

They sat at a table by a window that overlooked the grounds of the castle of Lupus. "Tell me about Vasht." Avon said.

"She was Reiss's woman."

"When will Reiss come here?"

Anna paused between mouthfulls of blood-red meat. "He is a prisoner."

Avon was startled. "What?"

"He killed two leaders of the Council. An attempted coup of some sort."

"Their names?"

"Blanca was one. The other was his lover, Pel Gros."

Avon wiped his mouth with a napkin. "Gros was one of those three who connived in the matter of my father's death."

"Who is the other?"

"Axel Reiss himself."

They were both alarmed by a sudden loud knocking on the door. Indicating that Anna should remain still and silent, Avon crossed the room, approached the door, turned a key and opened it.

"I hope I'm not intruding," Maco said.

Avon smiled and stepped aside. "Come in."

"Thank you." Maco stepped over the threshold and, closing the door behind him, Avon led him to the table.

Anna stood.

"Introductions are unnecessary," Maco said to Avon.

"We know each other well." His pebble glasses gleamed. "I take it you are reconciled?"

Avon said nothing, but he poured their guest a glass of wine.

"There appears to have been a misunderstanding." Maco said. "News of Sabbath's death had preceded us. As he was once an admired member of the Death Squad elite and it was learned that you had had something to do with his death, his comrades expressed, shall we say, annoyance. They decided you should not escape unpunished. Hence their playful antics upon our arrival."

Avon rubbed his sore face. "Playful is not the word I would have chosen."

Maco smiled. "Tomorrow, you will be inducted into the family. However, there is a complication. You probably know from Anna here that Axel Reiss has been arrested for the murder of Blanca and Pel Gros."

Avon nodded. He stood quite still. He thought he knew what was coming.

"Reiss has elected to defend himself. He has requested trial by combat." Maco sniffed. "It's an ancient and barbaric rite." He smiled thinly. "Civilization has come a long way, hasn't it?" He looked from one to the other. "Vasht has nominated Avon as his opponent."

"Perhaps my membership of the Seventh family will be shortlived." Avon said drily.

"We must make every effort to ensure that you survive the encounter." Maco said significantly.

Anna stepped between them. "Maco, can we trust you?"

"With what?"

"Our lives."

"A heavy responsibility."

161

"We wish to escape the Federation."

Maco smiled patronizingly. "That is a virtual impossibility."

"We intend to run to the Children."

Maco appeared stunned.

Avon, who trusted no one, was appalled by Anna's confession. He watched their visitor carefully, prepared to kill him if any thought of betrayal seemed to cross his mind. Maco remained impassive.

After a while, he exhaled slowly. He looked at them both admiringly. "A bold plan," he said.

"But feasible," Anna said excitedly.

"You would need a great deal of money." Maco said. Then realization dawned and he smiled broadly. "Money that the Seventh family could provide."

"Will it?" Avon asked.

Maco shook his head. "No." Reflected light danced on his glasses. "Of course, with my assistance, it would be possible to obtain the documentation necessary for a trip to Jupiter. From there, I could arrange that we safely reach the sanctuary of the Children."

"We?" Avon said.

"If I am to assist," Maco spread his hands in a gesture of finality, "I could not stay behind. The Federation would exact hideous retribution."

Avon eyed him suspiciously. "Why should you give up everything you have here in order to help us?"

"Pah! I have very little. I am subject to the whims of Vasht and any other puffed-up member of the High Council. I am also a slave to the families."

"Then, you will help us?" Anna asked.

"And help myself."

"How do we get hold of the money?" Avon asked, ever practical.

"That will be up to you. Once I have introduced you

162

to the banking house, you must find a way to enter the computer programs and syphon off what we require. You must do it in such a way that we will gain a few days grace before the embezzlement is discovered."

"What makes you think I'm capable?"

Maco smiled his secret smile. "I've been given access to all information concerning your aptitudes and skills. Remember, I'm supposed to be a trusted employee of Vasht and Axel Reiss. I know you have talent."

"I can't help feeling," Avon said coolly, "that these circumstances have arisen a little too fortuitously. Why do I imagine I am being manipulated?"

Maco smiled disparagingly. "You are a cautious man. But ask yourself why anyone here would care to manipulate you. The Federation is all powerful. At the moment, Vasht is all powerful. She could eliminate you like that!" He snapped his fingers. "Anyway, all this could be academic. Our little scheme could go awry. There is the matter of your stand-off with Reiss. If he kills you, we are all three dead!"

"Don't fight him," Anna said urgently. "Let's run before they make you."

"Difficult," Maco said.

"But not impossible!" Anna was angry, seemingly protective of her lover.

"You know it is impossible," Avon said softly.

Maco smiled. "You see? He wants to fight. He wants to kill Reiss."

"I have to kill him," Avon said.

Anna appeared to accept defeat.

"I might be able to help you," Maco said matter-of-factly. "In studying your file, I was stuck by Sabbath's comments about you when you faced danger and, apparently, superior odds. He noted, with some admiration I thought, that you are prepared to use any

163

and every means to achieve the right result. With Axel Reiss, believe me, you are outmatched. I can arrange something to tilt the balance in your favor. I hope you're not too proud or chivalrous to refuse my help."

Avon looked at him, his face expressionless.

"I take it from your silence that you accept?" Maco said. "Had you refused, then our other plan would be finished before it had begun."

"When has Vasht decided the combat will take place?" Avon asked.

"In a little less than an Earth month from now."

"In the meantime?"

"In the meantime, you are a valued member of the Seventh family. Privy to all its financial secrets." Maco helped himself to more wine. He raised his glass in a silent toast, then drained it.

Anna sat on the couch. Both she and Maco looked steadily at Avon. After a long pause, Maco smiled and said, "We three could be a formidable combination."

Avon, ever watchful, ever suspicious, smelling conspiracy, always untrusting, said, "But which of us holds the key?"

7

The Earth city of Lupus, cradle of Federation civilization, perched on a great mountain, was a brilliant example of architectural genius old and new. Buildings evoking memories of bygone eras stood closely ranked with modern hi-tech edifices that in no way overwhelmed them.

To an outsider, an alien perhaps, the city would

appear to be fitting to the greatness of which *Homo sapiens* is capable.

Within, however, the species bustled about like ants on a hill. Man here was bloated by corruption. Quivering with greed, envious and cruelly eager, most inhabitants sought their own ends with a ruthlessness and carelessness of others that would have made Rome under Nero seem idyllic.

Maco, true to his word, introduced Avon to the system. The young man, a product of that very system, was undismayed.

The Seventh family's banking interests were housed in one of the newer buildings. Meagrely staffed, the financial house depended on its computer banks. Many of them of advanced design.

Provided he had the skill, the time and Maco as his sentry, Avon would enter their programs and disarrange them to his advantage.

Maco made certain that he alone instructed his protégé, that they would not require the assistance of others, that they would not socialize. This arrangement seemed acceptable to the family.

Avon studied the computer models. He read and researched. All the while, the machinery twinkled at him. Only the soft hiss of its workings disturbed his concentration.

At last, after some twenty days, he found a way.

He explained his scheme to Maco. He tapped one of the older computer models with his fingers. "I learned on one of these at the Iron School," he said. "It's possible, if properly conceived, to overlay one or more of its programs."

Maco sniffed. "Assume that I am ignorant. Keep your explanation simple," he said.

Avon smiled. "I intend to insert an alternative

165

program. I will superimpose it on a present one. Rather like using a transfer paper or rubbing brass. Of course, there are safety devices, booby traps. But, thanks to you, I have had access to all the computer manuals and I have found a method of disarming it. What I will do is lift off the first program and mingle it, as it were, with my own. Naturally, the computer will be confused and react accordingly. Because I've succeeded in disarming it, it will accept my insertion as legitimate and adjust to the new input. The original program will alter, assuming some of the characteristics of mine. It will continue to function quite normally, but with an almost imperceptible difference. The new program will instruct this computer to talk to its brother on Jupiter. It does that anyway. The information it will pass on will cause small amounts of currency to be syphoned off into a bogus company. It's really very simple. The Seventh family would be expected to conduct business with any company prepared to deal in funds obtained from the drug market."

Maco nodded approvingly. "Entry into that forbidden arena is long overdue. Made possible by the timely departure of Pel Gros."

Avon patted the machine as if it were a faithful dog. "There are other models similar to this. I will insert simultaneous programs. By the time we reach Jupiter, the combined efforts of these computers will have placed a sizeable sum with our non-existent but apparently legitimate company."

"How much?" Maco couldn't restrain his curiosity and excitement.

"Upwards of five hundred million credits."

Maco whistled through his teeth. "Enough to buy ten Starships."

"Enough to buy sanctuary from the Children."

"Quite! Can you be sure this will go undetected?"

"For a while. Look at it this way. What do you possess in Federation credits?"

Maco looked foxy. "Approximately two hundred thousand."

"There! You say, 'approximately.' It may be two hundred thousand and one. You are unlikely to concern yourself if that 'one' does not appear in your accounts. I have instructed the computer to transfer small sums from every account in the system. A credit here, perhaps two credits there. Once accumulated, our rich account is created."

Maco laughed. "Ingenious!"

"Hardly!" Avon said dismissively. "It's been done before. In fact, it wouldn't surprise me if it wasn't being done right now. Not on the same scale perhaps. There's no doubt that I will be found out sooner or later. There are no fools here. But, with your help, when I am discovered, I'll be long gone and well out of Federation reach."

Maco looked around furtively, but they were unobserved. "The date for the combat is set," he said. "Once you have killed Reiss, I will arrange for you to be lifted out of the combat zone and brought back here to Lupus. We will meet at an address I will give you. Anna will join us there. Then we'll take flight to Jupiter. Now, listen carefully. The combat is scheduled to last three days. If neither man is dead by then, the Iron Guard will kill both of you. Those are the rules. You must ensure that you win on the first day. By the time it becomes known we have fled to Jupiter, it will be too late for Vasht or anyone else to do anything about it."

"That doesn't seem long enough." Avon said.

"Trust me!"

Avon looked at him, his eyes hardened. "It would seem I have no choice. Don't betray my trust. You would not appreciate the consequences."

Maco smiled placatingly. He touched Avon's arm, the gesture paternal. "I'm in this as much as you are."

Someone was walking over to them.

"How long will it take to insert the fraudulent programs?" Maco asked in a whisper.

Avon whispered back, "I've already done it."

Another employee of the financial house, a member of the family, drew closer. He was about Avon's height, age and build. He had the face of a choirboy. He was called Tynus.

"Vasht wants to see you." Tynus said. His eyes, like a snake's, flicked from Avon to Maco and back again. "I hope your enterprise is thriving," he added.

Avon nodded and smiled coldly. "And yours."

Tynus frowned, then reassumed his angelic expression, bowed to each in turn and backed away.

"He knows?" Maco was aghast.

"He suspects."

"How?"

"Because he's up to exactly the same tricks. And he knows I know."

"Will he keep silence?"

"Long enough for us to do what we have to do. We have an unspoken agreement. I'm doing him a favor by pretending not to know what he's up to. He's prepared to return the compliment."

"I don't like the look of him," Maco said.

"Funnily enough, he said exactly the same thing about you!"

Maco smiled. "Still, I might find a use for him. In the meantime, we must not keep Vasht waiting. Come with me."

Avon obeyed and the two men rode a monorail to the castle grounds. The officer who had beaten Avon on the day they first arrived at Lupus was there to meet them. He escorted them into the building, along the wide marbled corridor to the Council chamber.

Vasht, seated at the great desk beneath the Bosch painting, rose to greet them. She dismissed the officer with a gesture bordering on contempt. Her eyes narrowed as she studied Avon. "I'm sorry we have not met before," she said courteously. "I've been busy."

"Murder and mayhem can be time consuming." Avon said.

Vasht smiled. "You may leave us Maco."

"But!"

"But me no 'buts.' Leave!"

Maco, after a moment's agitated hesitation, obeyed.

Vasht perched on the edge of the desk, lit a long cigar and blew smoke rings in the air.

"That's a bad habit," Avon said.

"It's not my only one!" She fluttered her eyelashes.

Avon smiled.

"You strongly resemble your father," Vasht said.

"I never knew him."

"No, of course not. Have you ever seen Axel Reiss?" she asked coyly.

"No."

"He too resembles your father."

Avon tensed. "In what way?"

"They were half-brothers. Didn't you know?" Vasht said innocently.

Although the day was warm, Avon felt chilled to the marrow. He could not bring himself to answer.

"Ironic isn't it?" Vasht continued. "I must admire Axel. He has used the Universe as his battleground for the conduct of a family feud."

"Why?" Avon's voice croaked.

Vasht frowned. "If you kill him, you may find out. If not, you may never know." She stubbed out her cigar. "Tomorrow, you will be transported to the killing zone," she said. "It is in the North, where your father died. Where he died by Axel's hand." Her eyes flashed like diamonds, challenging him.

Avon did not react.

Vasht seemed disappointed. "Reiss is there already. You have three days to resolve the combat. After that, the Iron Guard will hunt you down and kill you. If you should win, be at an appointed place with evidence of Reiss's death and you will be welcomed back into Federation society as a valued member."

Avon snorted.

Vasht looked up sharply. "That is a rule of the game," she said tersely. "In the even that you do win, it's a rule I'd like to break. Unfortunately, I am bound as you are."

Avon stood quite still as Vasht eased herself off the edge of the desk and walked round him as if assessing his value in a slave market. "For what it's worth," she said finally, "I think you'll lose."

Avon grabbed her arm and pulled her to him. She struggled, but his grip was like iron. "There are forces gathering to oppose you," he said quietly. "When I win, your lover and protector will be dead and in hell. I suspect you will join him there quite soon." He released her and pushed her away from him. For a moment, they faced each other like two cats in an alley, ready to dispute each other's territory.

Vasht smiled. "Like father, like son," she said.

"But not like dear uncle!" Avon replied.

"A pity."

Avon smiled. "You'd like to play both ends against

the middle, wouldn't you? Whoever wins in the North, you would like to have him on your side. I could become your creature in place of Reiss. I'm younger, I might last longer in the service of your purposes. But you could never trust me. Reiss is a better bet for you."

Vasht sighed. "I wish we had met before. You're right, of course. My days are numbered. The old Federation is crumbling about us. To be replaced by those with a liberal conscience. Conscience makes for cowards. In time, someone like me will seize power again. And so it will go on."

"It's not a very edifying prospect."

Vasht laughed, then was silent for a while. She turned away from him, walked to a tall window and looked out. "You had better leave," she said. Then added in a whisper, "Or stay if you will."

She whirled round. Avon had gone.

8

The heliplane flew low over the snowbound wastes. The pilot was the same Death Squad officer who had kicked Avon into consciousness and who had later introduced him to Vasht. His name was Raher.

Avon sat beside him in the narrow cockpit of the plane. He was dressed in a black coverall patched with leather. For the moment, he was unarmed. Only when he left the aircraft would Raher pass to him his twin-bladed knife with serrated edge.

Axel Reiss, deposited the previous day some hundred kilometers to the East, would be similarly armed. On a given signal, the two combatants were required to march to meet each other. The rules of the game were strict on these matters.

"In three days," Raher was saying, "I will land close by the ice obelisk. We fly near it. I'll point it out to you. The victor must rendezvous with me there. If no one comes within six hours of the appointed time, the Death Squad will be ordered in and whoever is still alive, perhaps both of you, will be hunted down. It's as well to be clear on this point. However, I expect Reiss to finish you quickly," he sneered.

Avon was studying the terrain beneath them.

"If you win," Raher went on, "You must bring me evidence to confirm your success."

"Such as?"

"Why not bring me Reiss's head? He brought your father's to Vasht!"

Avon turned his head very slowly and stared at him like a basilisk.

Raher, disconcerted, swung the controls so that the aircraft ducked and dived before resuming a steady course. Neither man spoke again until they reached their destination, some four hours flying time from Lupus.

They were visiting the exact spot where Reiss had slaughtered Rogue Avon more than twenty Earth years before. Nothing had changed.

Raher set the heliplane down on the soft, glistening carpet of snow and Avon jumped out of the cockpit onto the ground. The pilot threw him his sheathed knife. Immediately he had done so, he revved the machine's engines, reactivated its rotors and took off. Dipping the nose of the plane in salute, he flew off in the direction from whence they had come.

Avon stood alone in the midst of a white, wide space. Dressed in black, he stood out like a monument. A perfect target.

However, he knew that Reiss was a hundred kilometers away. Even if he was nearer, he would not have a long gun.

Avon looked westward. Some six kilometers distance was a stand of fir and pine trees.

"Find cover in the tress." Maco had said. "Reiss will be expecting you to move towards him so that you can fight at some halfway point. Don't! Stay where you are and make him come to you."

"How can you be sure of the place?" Avon had asked.

Maco had smiled his secret smile. "If Reiss has a weakness, I can guess what it is. There's a streak of sentiment in him. He will be glad to kill you on the ground where he killed your father. Logic! He and Vasht have arranged this together and Reiss calls the tune in that duet."

"So, he'll expect me to wait?"

"Yes."

"What if you're wrong about the location?"

"Then you have a problem that you will have to solve yourself. But I'll wager my life I'm right!"

Avon had smiled wryly. "Actually, it is my life you are wagering!"

Now he silently complimented Maco. His had been an educated guess that Avon, in his own heart, knew would be accurate.

He sat and waited. Silent, still and watchful, he allowed five hours to pass before the distant drone of a small heliplane's engines caused him to spring to his feet. Within minutes, the aircraft appeared as a mere speck in the far sky but, rapidly approaching him, it soon assumed its proper proportions.

The craft had been selected by Maco because it was

173

the smallest available and capable of avoiding most detector systems.

There was no way its pilot could fail to see Avon's black garbed figure silhouetted against the white background of snow.

The plane hovered close by, tilted slightly and a roll of canvas fell from its cockpit to the ground.

The pilot dipped the aircraft and, through a glass cocoon, Avon saw Tynus was at the controls. His fellow conspirator smiled angelically, then pulled hard on a lever in front of him and the plane jumped like a flea into the sky. It turned and sped away.

"It's an excellent plan," Maco had said. "The rules are very strict and command utmost respect. No one would dream that you would cheat."

"Rules are made to be broken," Avon had replied.

He ran across the snow and retrieved the bundle. It was not heavy and he continued running until, breathless, he reached the stand of trees.

He slit the canvas with his twin-bladed knife and discovered that the roll contained a compass, a small phial of nitroglycerine and an old-fashioned, six projectile hand gun which was fully loaded. There was also a brief message from Maco. In stark lettering, his mentor had written: "Beware Steljuks!"

Avon shivered involuntarily. He knew what Steljuks were. Half man, half beast, nomadic snow dwellers.

All the equipment with which he had now been provided was wrapped in a light coverall similar to the one he was wearing. With one important difference—it was white.

Avon stripped and exchanged one garmet for the other. Despite the fact that it was a dry, bright day, during the few moments he was naked, he felt a terrible chill.

When he was prepared, he once more settled down to wait.

He had now been in the North for six hours. According to the scheme that he and Maco had concocted, he could allow himself eighteen more in which to kill Reiss.

If his opponent was as crafty as he had surmised, he would not wait for Avon to make a move towards him. After all, he had been deposited one hundred kilometers distant a full twenty-four hours before. If Avon was willing to bend the rules of the engagement, Reiss would certainly follow suit and set out after his prey a full day ahead of schedule. Thus, he had had thirty hours grace. It would not be long before he put in an appearance.

Avon found a place beneath overhanging branches of fir trees and buried himself in a mound of snow. To a casual observer, he was now a part of the landscape.

He calculated that his adversary would probably cover the ground at a rate of four kilometers an hour. Allowing him rest periods of six hours, he guessed Reiss would take one more hour to reach him. This was his first mistake. Reiss was already there.

Avon was disturbed by a slight rustling sound in the trees behind him. "Bastard!" he thought. He now knew that Reiss had moved much faster than anticipated and had circled around him. He waited, hardly daring to breathe.

"Did you really think I'd fall for that old trick?" A deep voice called out.

Axel Reiss stepped out of the trees and stood facing his hideout. Not more than fifty metres away, he was hefting his double-edged knife, which glittered in the sunlight.

Almost shamefaced, Avon stood and brushed clinging

175

snow from his clothing.

"That's better," Reiss said. "Now I can see you properly."

Clearly surprised by the fact that Avon was wearing white when he should have been wearing black, Reiss took a few steps away from him. His eyes searched all around. Satisfied that they were alone, he relaxed slightly. "Come closer," he said, beckoning Avon forward.

Almost in spite of himself, Avon obeyed, his knife at the ready.

"So!" Reiss hissed. "Our moment has come."

Avon eyed him warily. It was if he was studying an older version of himself.

Axel Reiss smiled and any resemblance between the two men faded and was gone. "Will you make the first move or shall I?" Reiss asked mockingly.

Despite the warmth provided by his coverall, Avon felt cold fingers of fear spreading across his spine. The game of death was about to begin.

"How like your father are you," Reiss said. "The strong, silent type. We are about to discover just how strong."

Avon said nothing. He did not move a muscle.

Reiss, brandishing his knife, took a step towards him.

Avon produced the six projectile gun.

Reiss seemed rooted to the spot. "That's not allowed," he said politely.

Avon squeezed the trigger and the gun spat his reply. To his astonishment, the bullet, striking Reiss at about waist height, recocheted from his body, whining away into the air. Reiss staggered backwards from the impact, but was otherwise unharmed.

Avon fired again and the gun jammed.

Reiss was on him in an instant. Their knives locked

together, the two men fell to the ground and rolled like deadly lovers in the snow. Avon kicked out savagely and Reiss fell away from him. Avon's left arm smashed against his throat, but Reiss too kicked out and caught Avon a blow in the groin that caused a searing pain reminiscent of his first encounter with Raher.

Both men sprang to their feet and crouched in the classic knifefighter's stance. They circled each other. The gun, which had fallen from Avon's grasp, lay in the snow some few meters distant.

Reiss feinted and lunged. Avon parried, but Reiss came forward again very quickly, ducked under his guard and crashed him to the ground.

Avon kicking out with all the strength he could muster, connected with Reiss's chest and hurled him into the air.

Reiss landed like a cat and, as Avon scrambled to his feet, thrust the knife towards him and slashed him across his left arm. Blood stained the perfect white of the coverall.

Avon sprang back, Reiss in hot pursuit. Their blades clashed and sparks flew. Both men, breathless, stood facing each other, not more than two meters apart. Avon was standing on the gun. He lunged and Reiss stepped back. In a micro second, Avon snatched up the weapon and levelled it. Faint from his wound, his aim was unsteady, his vision blurred.

"That won't work," Reiss said casually.

Avon shook his head to clear it. Flourishing his knife, Reiss darted forward. Avon fired. There was a deafening roar and Reiss, an expression of sweet surprise on his face, was flung to the ground, blood spurting from his breast.

Avon stepped forward and straddled his fallen opponent. He levelled the gun once more. Reiss looked up at him and smiled. Avon shot him in the head.

As the echoes of the sound of their conflict faded away, an awful silence descended.

Avon took his knife and cut away Reiss's clothing. He saw the metal girdle that had substituted for manhood. It had been scored and dented by the first bullet.

Avon sat in the snow with the naked corpse and wept.

Later, he took the phial of nitrogylcerine, broke it and fired the body with the liquid. He used branches and twigs from pine and fir trees to boost the flames. A crooked pillar of smoke climbed into the sky.

This was a prearranged signal. This was how Tynus would locate him.

The fire consumed Reiss's body. The smoke grew dense as there was no wind to disperse it.

After a while, he heard again the drone of an engine and the tiny heliplane came into view.

Avon stood clear of the trees. The plane was approaching from the South. To the east, studding the horizon, were a dozen or more grotesque figures. Steljuks!

Tynus put the plane down some three hundred meters away. The Steljuks, if that was what they were and it was unlikely they would be anything else, charged towards it.

With great coolness, Avon ejected the faulty cartridge from his gun. He had three shots left. He went down on one knee, took careful, steady aim and fired in rapid succession. Two of the fast approaching figures fell, but the others came on without hesitation. Avon dashed for the heliplane.

Tynus, sensing the danger, began to lift off. Avon ran as fast as he could. It was touch and go whether the Steljuks would reach the aircraft before he did. He leapt forward and, just as the machine drifted lazily into the air, he grabbed one of its landing skis and clung on for dear life.

The heliplane rose vertically.

Avon looked down. The Steljuks were directly beneath him, but he was beyond their reach. The plane, its engines snarling, turned away, gained height and settled to its course.

Avon's hands gripped the ski like iron clamps. He prayed to an unknown god for deliverance.

Slowly, desperately, with enormous effect he dragged himself upwards. At last, he was able to straddle the ski. The heliplane, unbalanced by his weight, tilted dangerously. The ground beneath was a blur as the craft rushed over it. The sky above was still and blue and cold. Avon gritted his teeth and hauled himself upwards until, his fingers cracked and bleeding, he managed to crawl into the cockpit.

"Sorry about that," Tynus said. "I didn't like the look of your friends."

Avon gasped for breath. His left warm was limp. He had lost a good deal of blood. Every fiber of his being shuddered with pain.

"Congratulations!" Tynus said. "You've won. And to the victor must go the spoils."

"Nobody wins." Avon said hoarsely. But Tynus didn't hear him.

9

The rains had come and Lupus was shrouded in mist. This suited Avon and Tynus admirably.

Zig-zagging the aircraft through sentinels of rock carved out of the jagged mountains, Tynus skillfully maneuvered their way past attack detection devices and landed them safely. They were in a quiet location, designated by Maco, close to the business sector of the capital.

Avon had managed to staunch the blood that flowed from his arm wound and, although his hands were like bloody claws from the effort of trying to hold on to the heliplane's ski, he could still use them.

Once landed, Tynus helped him by providing clean water and by applying a transparent healing paste to the exposed cuts.

A steady drizzle and dusky clouds combined to obscure a fitful crescent moon. It was a dark night.

Before they parted company, Tynus said, "My life is in your hands. If your enterprise should fail and you are closely questioned—I mean, tortured—can I trust you not to reveal my activities in the banking system and the assistance I've given you in cheating the combat?"

"Any man has his breaking point," Avon said.

"You are not any man."

Avon smiled slightly. "You have my word."

"Good enough!"

Tynus did not offer to shake hands. He nodded, smiled and walked away through the rain, disappearing into the thick night. Avon was alone.

Once Tynus had gone and he was sure he could not follow, Avon set off for the house where he and Maco and Anna had agreed to meet.

Though the pain he felt was almost unbearable and the loss of blood had taken its toll, he found strength sufficient to allow him to traverse the wet city streets unobserved by occasional patrols of the Iron Guard police.

The house was in the heart of the financial district and was used by one of the corporations as basic accommodation for visiting functionaries or by anyone who was required to work through the night on Seventh family business.

Avon had a key, passed on to him by Tynus. He glanced around to make sure that no one else was in the vicinity. The streets were deserted. He let himself into the house and, having climbed a steep flight of stairs, found himself in a cheaply furnished apartment.

Having checked for unwanted visitors and surveillance, he made his way to a bathroom. Hot water scalded his aching body. Soothing creams sealed his scars.

Thoughtful and efficient, Maco had left him a full change of clothing and some food and drink, but, to his surprise, there was no weapon.

He must have occupied himself for close on an hour. When he entered the main room of the apartment, it was in darkness. A dim figure sat at a desk by a shaded window.

Avon tensed, ready to fight or run or both.

The figure switched on an elaborate lamp that stood on top of the desk. Avon breathed a sigh of relief. It was Maco.

"You caught me off guard," Avon said. "I didn't hear you come in."

"What happened?" Maco asked. His voice had a hard edge.

"I killed Reiss."

Maco smiled. "By fair means or foul?"

"What does it matter, so long as he's dead?"

"Quite!"

"Do you have the travel papers?" Avon asked.

Maco nodded.

"When should we expect Anna?"

Again Maco smiled. "I'm afraid she's not coming."

Avon's eyes narrowed. "Why not?"

"She's dead."

Avon stood quite still. Any observer would have said that he appeared unmoved. In reality, he felt as if his entire spirit was draining out of him. "How?" he croaked.

"What does it matter, so long as she's dead?" Maco said, at the same time producing a gun and pointing it straight at him. "Well done," he continued, his eyes unblinking behind his thick-lensed glasses, his attention completely devoted to Avon, his gun hand never wavering. "You have fulfilled your purpose. Now your usefulness is at an end."

Avon flopped against a wall, his face haggard. It seemed all his energy had drained away and that he was accepting defeat.

Maco stood and walked around the desk. "You have been the perfect dupe," he said.

Avon turned his face to the wall.

"Not only have you provided me with a bogus company on Jupiter," Maco continued, "a company with considerable assets, but you have also removed Vasht's champion from the scene. The Seventh family will ensure she is, shall we say, persuaded to retire from office and I, who have carried out this plan so neatly, will assume a position of importance hitherto unexpected. Thank you! Tynus, of course, about whom I know every compromising detail, will remain silent and subservient. However, your faithful and unsuspecting service must not to unrewarded. I've been toying with the idea of handing you over to Raher and the other Death Squad bullies but, on reflection, I must admit to having accumulated a certain amount of admiration for you. An admiration that Sabbath once shared. Look what happened to him! I think it would be dangerous to leave you alive. Don't you?"

Avon seemed overcome with anguish. "Was this planned right from our first meeting?" he asked.

"Yes."

"Did you kill Anna?"

Maco shrugged. "I left her to the tender mercies of others."

Avon shook his head wearily. "You had me completely fooled."

"Yes, didn't I? You're good Avon, very good, but as long as I'm around you'll always finish second."

Avon, using the wall at his back as a springboard, leapt forward. Maco fired. Avon, consumed by a terrible anger, ignored the bullet that tore into his clothing and smashed the gun from his hand. He and Maco grappled. Maco's glasses fell to the floor and were crushed under Avon's heel.

Avon took hold of Maco by the throat and, like a rabid dog, would not let go. Maco's sightless eyes bulged in their sockets. His face turned vivid red, then bruised purple. In no longer than it takes to tell, Avon strangled him and he was dead.

He lowered the body to the floor and sank, exhausted, into a chair. Blood oozed from a fresh wound in his side. He examined it carefully. The bullet had only grazed his flesh. The flow of blood was easily staunched.

Avon sat for a long time. Regaining his strength, he thought of Anna, of Reiss, of his mother, of the father he had never seen. He wished he had never been born.

Suddenly, the room was filled with light. Fierce neon searchlights were directed into the apartment so that every nook and cranny came into plain view. There was nowhere to escape their suffocating brilliance.

A disembodied voice spoke to him over a loud speaker. "You will walk down the stairs and through the open door into the street," the voice said. "You will lie down in the street and spread your arms and legs so that it can be seen you are unarmed. You have two minutes to comply. If you do not, a toxic gas will be released into the house and you will die in agony. Move!"

Avon had been as startled as a rabbit would have been when the lights came on, but now he was calm.

Maco was dead, Reiss was dead, everyone he had ever loved was dead. He stood, stepped over the corpse at his feet and walked down the stairs and into the street. He lay down on the wet ground. He raised his head slightly. Raher was smiling down at him.

"I expected Maco," the officer said. "I set a trap for a fox and snare a wolf. My masters will be pleased!" He laughed, but seemed unwilling to share the joke.

10

The cell was large enough and contained the usual amenities. Avon sat on a thin mattress that almost covered a metal cot.

Raher stood by the door. He smiled patronizingly. "I'm sorry for you. You don't deserve this," he said.

"We rarely get what we deserve," Avon replied, his voice a dull monotone.

"It would seem that your family has—had—an unfortunate weakness," Raher went on. "You are—

were—too easily gulled. Like son, like father! My professional respect for you notwithstanding, it is—was—a grievous fault."

"What happens now?" Avon asked.

"Certain influential members of the nine families asked for Vasht's removal from the High Council. She saw the writing on the wall and beat them to the punch. She slashed her wrists while in her bath and bled to death. A pity! She was a handsome woman. Maco, of course, was too ambitious. Ambition should be made of sterner stuff."

"Anna?"

Raher frowned. "What about her?"

"How did she die?"

Raher pursed his lips and looked thoughtful. "I don't know," he said cautiously. "Aren't you more interested in what's going to happen to you?"

Avon said nothing.

"Well, I'll tell you anyway," Raher said. "You are to be transported to a prison planet." He paused for a reaction. When there was none, he continued, "Newly acquired by the Federation, it could be described as the worst place in the Universe. A vote was taken and, by a narrow majority, your life was spared. But our masters are nothing if not subtle in their vengeance. They have condemned you to a living death."

Still Avon said nothing.

Raher, who clearly liked to talk, went on. "Of course, there's a certain amount of political turbulence at the moment. Human rights have become a major issue and the Federation is behaving with remarkable restraint. Nevertheless, you'll have a goodly number accompanying you to where you're going. Sooner or later we'll get back to normal and my kind will step out of the shadows to assume control."

185

"When do I leave?"

"Some time yet, I'm afraid. There's a major trial going on. One of those high-minded liberals who has appealed a little too effectively to the rabble conscience."

"The trial will be rigged, of course?"

"Of course."

"Then I'll probably meet this dissident."

"Oh, I don't think you and he will get along."

"In the meantime?" Avon asked.

"In the meantime—make yourself comfortable. Believe me, the time you spend here will seem like days in heaven compared to your ultimate destination? Paroch will take good care of you."

Avon concealed his surprise on hearing the name.

"Unlike you," Raher said, "Paroch, once a revolutionary, saw the error of his ways and returned to the Federation fold. You couldn't find a more eager convert to its absolutism."

"I doubt that I should look forward to meeting him," Avon said drily.

Raher laughed. "I'll leave you to reflect on what might have been," he said. "While I attend to what, for me, will be."

"You expect promotion?"

"Absolutely." Raher gave him a mocking salute and left him. The iron door of the cell thudded into place behind his receding back. It was as if Avon were suddenly entombed.

But, true to his word, the Death Squad officer left him plenty of time for reflection. He waited patiently for his inevitable meeting with Paroch.

After almost an Earth month had passed, he saw him.

Dressed as a junior officer in the Iron Guard, the

former courier for the Prospector on Nereid approached him when he was walking, slightly apart from other prisoners, in the prison exercise yard.

The Nereidian fell into step beside him and spoke softly, his lips barely moving. "Keep walking! Look downcast if you can manage it. As if I'm giving you a tough dressing down."

"I'll try."

"You're to be transported. But you know that."

"Yes."

"You won't like it."

"So I gather."

"There's little I can do to help."

"Why should you?"

Paroch smiled wanly. "For old time's sake? Starets, the Prospector, persuaded me to go over to the enemy. I think you inspired him. The cancer within the body politic does greater harm than attempts to destroy it from without. You've proved that to an extent."

"I'm flattered," Avon said.

Paroch snorted. "Don't be. I'll do what I can for you. If I give you only a slight chance of survival, I have a feeling you'll take it!"

Their next furtive conversation came when Paroch was detailed to brief Avon on his immediate future.

The prisoner was to be taken under heavy guard to the court of the Council and formally arraigned. The death penalty, as a sop to the liberalism currently in fashion, was to be commuted. But fraud coupled with extreme violence was a sufficient conviction to ensure his promised transportation from Earth for the rest of his life. Federation justice would be done.

On the way to the court, Paroch slipped Avon a small piece of stiff backed paper. Concealing it, Avon did not dare even to glance at it until certain he would be unobserved.

The Federation system of justice ran smoothly. Raher, with Paroch in attendance, plus an assortment of Iron Guards, escorted Avon from the court directly to the waiting prison spaceship. Many prisoners were already aboard, others were still being processed.

Raher watched the pathetic figures for a moment. "The beginning of the end for all of you," he said.

Avon did not speak. His expression was grim.

"I will now hand you over to the tender mercies of the prison officer of this ship." Raher said with relish. "Take my advice and keep a low profile. He has an unenviable reputation for cruelty."

"I'll bear that in mind."

Prison ship guards came to relieve Raher of his charge. "Goodbye," he said, "I won't wish you luck. Yours has just run out!"

Avon nodded. He cast a sideways glance at Paroch and winked.

The prison ship officers, weary of their task, but reasonably tolerant provided he caused them to no trouble, took him up the ramp that led into the main hold of the aircraft. Convicts were milling about searching for living space for the interminable, deadly journey to come.

Close to one of very few portholes, a big man was held in a chair by iron clamps. A guard nodded in his direction. "We expect trouble from that one."

"Why him in particular?" Avon asked.

"He's one of those human rights activists. A real rabble rouser. With a bit of bad luck, he won't last the trip. Behave yourself and you just might."

Avon nodded meekly.

Once left to his own devices, he found himself a quiet corner on the prison deck. No one seemed to be paying him any attention and he had seated himself in such a way that the surveillance monitors could hardly see what he was doing. He took out the blocked paper that Paroch had surreptitiously passed to him. Upon it was a diagram in miniature of the complete layout of the prison ship. There were details of all computers carried aboard, of all controls, of all surveillance techniques. It was an escaper's charter.

He looked around him. In the midst of a sad example of defeated, hopeless humanity, with the smell of fear and degradation in his nostrils, with the whimpers of discontent in his ears, for no apparent reason, Avon smiled.

THE END?